K-REX

L.Z. HUNTER

SEVERED PRESS
HOBART TASMANIA

K-REX

CHAPTER 1

The water in the stream was crisp, clear. It wasn't much deeper than two feet. The rocks and sand below were visible. There wasn't much of a current. The most dangerous aspect was the slippery rocks. Barefoot, the man let his toes curl over whatever he stood on for balance. His back hurt most. Standing bent forward for hours took a toll. He stood and stretched every few minutes. The pain hit the lower back. The muscles twisted into knots. The heat and humidity didn't help. If he were under the canopy, it wouldn't be as hot. Thankfully, a splash from the stream now and then cooled him off.

The jungle was alive around him. As the sun set, it would get louder. The chimps and bonobos shouted back and forth, working themselves up. The grunts and screams became more high-pitched and aggravated. That was normal. Owls hooted. Branches snapped now and then. The lions and hyenas were out, but they stepped carefully. It wasn't them breaking twigs.

Where the stream turned, and became slightly swifter, he panned for coltan. He swirled water and sand around, letting them drain leaving only chunks of minerals for picking through. He wore a canvas bag over his shoulder, and filled it with the coltan found. He kept the bag close. The militia robbed him often, or paid rates less than what the dig was worth. Either way, he and his family lost out. It didn't stop him, and although annoyed, he didn't let the theft make him angry. There was plenty of coltan. He could make up the lost money just adding extra working hours to his day.

Or evening.

He didn't like being away from home for long. Walking home in the dark was less than ideal. There was more than militia to fear. He'd never seen the giant Kasai Rex. The stories told sounded fabricated. He knew dinosaurs existed. The crocodiles in the rivers were proof of that. The crocs, however, were the only prehistoric animals he'd ever seen. Night-time was funny, though. After spending the entire day under the sun, the mind cooked. His imagination was like the nocturnal animals around him. Awake.

There was no fast way of moving through the jungle. Slow and safe was best. The moss-covered rocks were slippery. The thick vegetation needed machete cutting every few feet. Any temporary paths made were swallowed back up by the rainforest within days, overgrown and difficult to find to get through within a week. Tree roots existed simply to cause stumbling. They snaked across the covered ground, and were large enough that falling over them seemed likely. Low branches, usually wrapped up by snakes, or webbed by giant spiders forced people to bend lower, ducking left and right. And there were always things crawling around under fallen tree limbs and behind large plant leaves. Best way to prevent injury was giving yourself enough time so you have some daylight left to walk under, without feeling the urge to run.

He swished the water and sand out of his pan. The dull black mineral inside was coltan. It was just a few pebble-sized pieces. It was always just a few pieces, but once added with the others in his bag, the pieces became handfuls. A handful was equivalent to a couple of days' pay.

Those who mined deeper into the earth rather than panning streams found larger quantities of coltan, and larger sized chunks. Except land where coltan was excavated was bought up by companies from all over the globe. Men with guns protected the parcels. Even if a section of land wasn't owned, it didn't mean someone wasn't mining it. While he wouldn't mind bigger finds, he wasn't greedy.

The rustle came from several yards inside the forest. He looked toward the trees. The leaves, vegetation and setting sun was far too thick. He could barely see further than a foot into the thicket.

It was time to go. The nocturnal animals hunted this time of night. His wife would have dinner waiting for him at home. He would much rather have dinner with his family, than become dinner for a pack of hyenas.

He pulled open the strings on his bag, and fit his large, round and thin pan inside with the small amounts of coltan collected.

The rustle came again. Closer.

He pulled the machete from the sheath on his belt. Quick movement was never a good idea when being watched.

It happened fast. He saw the head of a female lion as the ground cover parted.

His breath caught in his lungs. His heart sank into his stomach.

The second lioness popped out of the trees beside the first.

The rustling must have been them running. They came at him, sprinting. Their paws were so large. The animals' eyes were opened so wide.

He tried not imagining the takedown. He planned on defending himself. He raised the machete with one hand. His other arm wrapped around the bag, as if the lionesses wanted his panning. He wasn't protecting the mineral. He was hugging himself.

He screamed as he began slashing the air with his long, curved blade.

The lionesses never made eye contact. They splashed through the stream, crossing it in two leaps and one bound. They were on the other side of the bank and back into the forest.

He stared at the tree line they'd entered. His machete lowered beside him, and breathed out a long, loud sigh. And laughed. Those lions were after prey. They had tunnel vision when it came to hunting. They weren't after him.

His laugh became a little louder, as relief passed through his entire body, and his muscles relaxed some. He had no intention of telling the family this story. His wife didn't like him panning anyway. It was one of the few ways of making a solid living in the Congo, just not one of the safest.

Turning around, he stopped.

It stood on the west bank, staring at him. He didn't move. His mouth went dry. He couldn't swallow.

When it blinked, the pupils became larger.

Lack of sunlight.

Its three toed claws looked sharp, like talons.

A noise came to his left. He turned his head slowly, and stopped when he saw what made it.

Peripherally, standing just in front of a tree was another one.

He had never seen them before.

There were the rumors and stories about the Kasai, but this. . .

The lions weren't after him because they'd been running away from something else. The lions were the prey. How often did that happen? Didn't matter if they were at the top of the food chain. When something chased them, they didn't hesitate. Instinct kicked in and they ran.

Lions ran fast.

His legs felt stiff, frozen. Every muscle in his back screamed in pain. He'd been standing, and bent over the last eleven hours. He was nearly forty years old. How fast could he run?

He backed up a step.

They watched him. Looked at each other. Looked back at him.

He knew his lips moved, but no words came out. He wanted to tell them to stay where they were. Everything was okay. He was just going to leave them alone now.

Not a sound escaped him.

Another step backward. His heel slipped on a rock. His boots were old. The traction was worn away. He lost his balance and his arms shot up, reaching out far left and far right. It worked, though. He didn't fall. Somehow he kept his feet. Smiling, he looked up. The smile vanished.

They were gone. Both of them. He looked around. Slow at first, and then his confidence built. They weren't anywhere around. The two lionesses would make a much better meal, he imagined. Maybe they just became curious seeing him straddling the stream. An anomaly is all. He'd confused them. They weren't interested in eating something new.

No one liked eating something new. Tried and true was always best. You eat something you never had before and you risk getting sick and upsetting the whole digestive process.

He couldn't help it. He felt good. Damned good. He had absolutely no idea what those things were, but he was going to be alive to talk about it. He'd lived in Africa all of his life. Moved to the Democratic Republic of the Congo seven years ago and spent most every day since in the forest panning for coltan. Countless times he now recalled scoffing the locals and their legends.

In the morning, he wasn't panning for coltan. He needed a gun.

The high-pitched squawk, followed by a guttural growl came from behind him. He didn't stop, nor did he look back. He just picked up the pace. He looked at his feet. He made each step carefully. He was not going to trip. He refused to fall.

If he didn't stop, he was all set. He walked with pure confidence.

His left had held onto the machete so tightly his black skin looked ashen, white. He knew he breathed too fast. His breaths were quick and shallow. The heat and humidity had nothing to do with the way his body perspired.

It was behind him. Its claws splashed in the water as it followed close behind.

Everything inside of him wanted to turn around. He would not give in. He did not look, would not look. He wanted whatever it was to think he didn't care, and that he wasn't afraid.

He was petrified.

The things he saw were not giants, like locals warned. It only meant they might be babies. If they were babies, where were the mothers? Worse, the fathers?

What if they were in their teen years?

Hormonal and crazy.

Did these things have puberty?

He was losing his mind. He knew it. The randomness of thoughts couldn't be stopped. They just filled and cluttered his mind. He had no way of sorting through them. Best he could do was push them aside after having thought them.

He almost screamed. His mind was berating him for having random thoughts.

He needed to focus on whatever was behind him.

He stopped walking.

Listened.

Waited.

He turned around.

They were matched in height. Head to head, and nose to nose.

It breathed heavily through its nostrils.

Something splashed into the water. He felt suddenly nauseated, and worried he might vomit. Moving just his eyes, he looked down into the stream. It was filled with blood, and intestines. The current attempted pulling it downstream.

He put his right hand over his stomach.

It was gone. A hole was there.

The thing had slashed him, disemboweling him. Strength gone, he fell to his knees. The creature in front of him shouted up at the darkening sky. He would have covered his ears with his hands. Instead he tried gathering guts and stuffing them back inside his body.

He knew something had bitten him.

His machete fell into the water beside him. It splashed cool water onto his leg. When he looked down, he knew he would not be picking it up. His hand was still attached to the machete handle, along with half of his arm. His head felt woozy. His balance teetered. Both legs became weak, as if his kneecaps had turned into jelly.

Looking to his left, he saw the second monster. Part of his body and cotton clothing was stuck between its teeth.

He opened his mouth to scream. It lunged for him, eating his face. He saw down the thing's throat as it bit into the sides of his head. He felt teeth crush skull, and finally the popping of his temples, and then. . .

CHAPTER 2

Louis Powell straightened the knot in his tie. He used his reflection on the closed elevator doors as a mirror. His stomach sank as the car rose. The bosses were on the twenty-second floor. He worked on the third. Except during orientation, he'd never been this high in the tower before. The message was on his desk. "Gary Brunson wants to see you in his office as soon as you get to work."

At first he thought it was a prank; one of the engineers pulling his leg. He checked with the software secretary since the note was in her delicate handwriting. She was a woman born lacking a sense of humor. A smile now and then was as far as it ever went. When asked, she confirmed the message's authenticity.

He wasn't relieved. A joke at his expense would have been better. Flying under the radar was how he preferred it. Come in, do his work, go home.

The elevator let out a soft ding. The car stopped. He looked ahead as the doors opened. The twenty-second floor lobby out-shined the street-level foyer. There were white marble floors, and spiral pillars. Floor to ceiling windows provided an exceptional view of the city skyline, and three rivers. The receptionist was in her fifties, pretty. Her blond hair was tied up in a bun. Light brown glasses sat on the end of her nose. The tan v-neck sweater was over a starched white dress shirt. "Mr. Powell, thank you for coming up. Mr.

Brunson and Ms. Warwick will meet you in the conference room."

He nodded, smiling. He had no idea where the conference room was, and pointed right. "This way?"

The woman stood up and walked around the counter. She wore tight black slacks, and high heels. "This way," she said, and went left. The hallway was wide, white, and bright. The lighting was soft. It didn't hurt his eyes. She stopped and opened a door. "There is coffee, water, bagels and danish. Help yourself while you wait. They shouldn't be long. Is there anything else I can get you?"

"I should be fine, thank you."

She nodded, and pulled on the door.

"Ah," he said. "Do you know what this is about?"

"They'll be with you shortly, Mr. Powell. Please, make yourself comfortable." She closed the door.

The windows in the conference room were also floor to ceiling. He walked up to them, hands in his pants pockets and took in the view. From here he could see the football, baseball and hockey stadiums. With a pair of binoculars, games could be watched from this window.

He looked at the clock on the wall. It was a little after eight. The refreshments were on a table in the back corner. He decided he'd fix himself a cup of coffee. As good as the fruit and cheese danish look, he passed. If he'd of taken one, the minute he bit into it, Gary Brunson would open the door. With sticky fingers he'd be forced to shake hands. No. He'd pass on the pastries.

Two cream. Two sugar. He used a stir stick, and picked up a napkin.

The conference table was glass with black legs. The chairs around it looked awkward and uncomfortable. He figured he'd stand until the boss joined him. He had no idea who Ms. Warwick was.

He placed the coffee cup on the napkin on the table and pulled out his phone. He accessed the Circuitz intranet website. He typed in Warwick. Hit enter.

She was in the Legal Department, inside counsel for employee relations.

Powell sat down. He didn't want to stand any longer. He set his phone beside his coffee, and dropped his head into his hand as he tried recalling any recent employee issues.

He'd fired employees for a number of reasons in the past. It always started with submitting the request for termination, with reasons attached. Legal reviewed the submission, and as long as there weren't any obvious issues, permission was granted. Issues only came up if the person fit into one of the state or federally protected classes.

It didn't mean a person couldn't be let go, it just meant the company ensured the employee wasn't fired because of the protected class they fit into. It became hairy at times. Powell knew documentation was key, and kept a journal recording most every interaction. The journal was discoverable, but he knew it was better covering his ass and protecting the company in a potential discrimination lawsuit, over letting everyone get burned and lose millions in paid out da*mages*.

Currently, he didn't have a pending termination request. Jobs were tough to find. Employees of Circuitz knew they had it good. Competitive pay and pretty good benefits made them better than most employers. People showed up, generally on time. Most worked past quitting time. When he was in the manufacturing part of the company, it was different. Supervising software engineers was a walk in the park in comparison. His people were professional. Quirky, but professional.

Was it him? Had he done something wrong?

He wondered if someone had filed a complaint. About what though?

He was single. Twenty-nine. He spent his days and evenings here, and went to bed early when home. He had zero social life outside of the job. What could he have done that caused someone to report him to legal?

If Gary Brunson and legal were involved, it must be bad. He just had no idea...what.

There was a knock on the conference room door, and then it opened.

He stood up, and ran his hand over his tie.

"Mr. Powell," Brunson said. He held out his hand as he stepped into the room.

"Mr. Brunson, sir." They shook hands.

"And this is Ms. Betty Warwick," Brunson said.

"Ms. Warwick." He shook her hand next.

She didn't say anything, just walked around the large table, set her briefcase down on the glass top and sat in a chair by the window.

"Please, sit down," Brunson said. "Have you tried the danish?"

"Had a big breakfast," Powell said, and patted his stomach. He thought if he had anything to eat now, he'd vomit. This reminded him of driving with a police car behind him. Even though he hadn't broken any traffic laws he couldn't help feeling guilty.

"Sit, then. Please," Brunson said.

The boss' suit was Italian, and cost more than Powell made in a month.

"Ms. Warwick?" Brunson pointed at the refreshments.

"I'm all set, Gary," she said.

Powell watched the dynamics. She used his first name. He'd called her Ms. Warwick. What was up with that?

Brunson snatched a bottle of water. He sat at the head of the table with the lawyer on his right, Powell on the left.

"I bet you're wondering why we've called you up." Brunson said. He opened the plastic bottle, took a long drink and set the bottle down. He smiled.

"I'm curious, yes."

"You've been with us, how long?" Brunson said.

"About seven years, Mr. Brunson."

"And you like it? You like working at Circuitz?"

He nodded, maybe a little too vigorously. "I do, sir. Yes."

"Good. Good. That's what we like to hear, isn't it, Ms. Warwick?"

She didn't reply, but worked the dials unlocking her briefcase. She depressed the snap-releases, and opened the lid.

"You have a bachelor's degree in software engineering, correct?"

"I do. Yes."

"You had a double major, I believe?"

"Geology," Louis Powell said. He leaned forward, not sure where the conversation was headed. Regardless, he wanted the big boss to know he had his full, undivided attention. "Just something I've always enjoyed. I was taking extra classes anyway. A double major was right there, so I finished taking what was needed."

"Commendable. Very admirable," Brunson said.

The smile made Powell a little apprehensive. "Well, I don't know about all of that. Just a personal choice, really."

"Did you aspire to work in the field, going on digs and the like?"

"As a kid, a young man, I think part of me did," Powell said.

"And what changed?" Brunson said.

Louis couldn't help watching Ms. Warwick. Her expression hadn't changed. She was writing on a yellow legal pad. Was she taking notes on the conversation? Why would she? His degree had no bearing on his job. Did it?

"I suppose reality changed."

"Reality?"

"I'm not one for writing grants. Digs need sponsoring. I work for everything I have. If I'd been independently wealthy, maybe I'd have explored the option after graduation. Sooner or later though, I'd have come to the same decision," he said.

"Same decision?"

"Software engineer. It's what I'm meant to do," Powell said.

Brunson laughed. "You think telling me what I want to hear, is what I want to hear."

Powell offered up a thin smile. "I'm really not sure what is going on, sir. And I'll admit, I'm a little apprehensive."

"Apprehensive? Louis, you have no reason to be. Trust me." Brunson nodded at Ms. Warwick.

She reached into her briefcase.

"Do you know what this is, Mr. Powell?"

Louis. Mr. Powell. The boss was all over the place. It caught him off guard.

Ms. Warwick produced a blue velvet cloth. She unwrapped it. A rock was inside. She set it down on the table.

Powell pointed at it. "May I?"

He pulled the rock close. He turned it over in his hands, and looked at it closely.

"Do you know what it is?" Brunson said, again.

Powell set the rock down on the velvet. "It looks like coal, the dull, black part embedded in the rest of the sediment."

He ran a finger over it, looked at his finger tip. "But I don't think it is. I'm not sure what it is."

"It's your paycheck, Mr. Powell." Brunson said. "It is our paycheck. The black rock in there is coltan."

Coltan. He should have known. He picked up the rock again and studied it more closely. "I've never seen it in raw form like this before. It's a dull, metallic ore."

"You know something about it?"

"Yes, sir."

"Tell me what you know," Brunson said.

"Well, I know that it is often referred to as the blood diamond of the technology world. It looks just like gravel, which was why I said coal. Only because, I guess I couldn't see you calling me up here to show me a piece of gravel." Powell set the rock down again. "The parts of this metallic ore are used in circuit boards, cell phones, video game consoles, e-readers, missiles, jet engines..."

Brunson sat forward, his arms on the table. "Exactly. It's used in capacitors, and tiny components that are essential in managing the flow of current in just about any and every electronic device that exists. The bigger question is, do you know what it is worth?" Powell shook his head. "I don't."

Brunson dropped a finger on a corner of velvet and slid the rock over. "The Tantalite, and Niobium content, as well as radioactive levels are what is looked at when it comes to pricing."

"Radioactive?"

"This particular piece has low, low radioactive levels. No worries," the boss said.

Powell *was* worried. He absently rubbed his palms over his suit pants. "I see," he said.

"A thousand a pound. If we're lucky. We pay one thousand dollars for every pound of coltan delivered. Do you know how many pounds of coltan we purchase a year? A month?"

Powell shrugged, and arched his eyebrows. "I don't, sir."

"A lot. Astronomical amounts. If Circuitz was a person, this ore is the lifeblood," he said, holding the rock up as a prop.

Powell was at a loss. He still had no idea why he was here. The only lines he could draw were his degree in geology, and the fact the company used coltan. He kept his mouth shut, and waited.

"We want to promote you, Louis. We want to make you a project manager. How many people do you supervise currently?"

"Seventeen," Powell said, without hesitation. He knew his staff as well as he knew most of his family. They were also equally as dysfunctional. Like family, though, they were his.

"Wonderful. Wonderful," Brunson said. "Ms. Warwick has the legal documents for you to look over and sign. There is a fifteen percent raise involved, if that is acceptable?"

"Ah, fifteen percent? Yes. Fifteen percent is acceptable," Powell said, running numbers inside his head. What clogged the thought process was legal. He'd signed confidentiality and non-compete clauses when hired. He knew what was expected of him as an employee.

"That's what I hoped to hear."

"And the legal documents?" Powell pointed at Ms. Warwick.

"We have an additional life policy form, compensation package, and enhanced confidentiality releases that require your signature," Ms. Warwick said, she stood up and walked over. She set a manila folder down in front of him. There were pages and pages of contracts, and supporting documentation. Sticky arrows were affixed anywhere his signature or initials were needed.

"What is the project?" Powell said, his eyes blurred looking over the paperwork. He couldn't concentrate on reading what was in front of him with Brunson staring.

"You are going to be in charge of our coltan supply," Brunson said.

In charge of the coltan supply? Could the geology degree really be paying off? His father would never believe this. "In charge of it, sir?"

"We know you are not married."

"I'm not."

"No kids."

"True."

"And your parents are retired and living in Florida."

It was kind of creepy. "You are right," Powell said.

"Based on everything, we believe you are the best company candidate for the project manager position. I mean if you aren't interested, we can go to the next person on the list," Brunson said.

They had a list? "I'm interested. I am," he said, picked up a pen and started signing and initialing as Ms. Warwick turned pages and pointed.

Brunson stood up. "Congratulations, Mr. Powell. I'm excited to have you on the team."

They shook hands. He excused himself, leaving Louis alone with the attorney.

Powell stopped when he noticed forms on traveling and Visa application. "Work Visa? Am I going somewhere?"

"We don't mine for coltan in Pittsburgh, Mr. Powell," Betty Warwick said.

"So, ah, where am I headed?"

"To where the coltan is," she said. "Sign here."

He signed. "Like a process factory? Where is it, Mexico? China?"

"You're not going to a factory, Mr. Powell. You are going where the ore is mined."

Where it is mined? "I don't know where it's mined from. Where am I going?"

He took the papers from the attorney and flipped through the pages, scanning them more closely. He saw his destination just as the lawyer explained.

"You have agreed to go to central Africa, Mr. Powell. For three months. You will be stationed in the Democratic Republic of the Congo."

CHAPTER 3

Louis Powell sat behind his desk, and stared blankly at his opened laptop. He wasn't positive how he felt, but thought shell-shocked might best describe it. The fifteen percent raise was substantial. Spending three months in a rain forest, in a third world country was far less appealing. Wasn't there some kind of war going on over there?

The light knock on his door seemed accidental. He looked up. A young woman stood in the doorway. She wore a grey suit, black glasses, auburn hair hung just above her shoulders. "Can I help you?"

"Actually, can I help you? I'm Claire Askew," she entered the office, hand extended.

Powell stood up, shook it.

"I'm your assistant," she said. "Mr. Brunson assigned me to you a few days ago. I start today."

Louis laughed as he sat back down. "You are *my* assistant? I'm going to be in Africa for the next year. I'm not sure how much help you'll be. I think they might have played a quick one on you."

"The Congo. I know. I'm coming with you," she said.

"You're going to Africa, too?" Powell said. Wonderful.

"I am. And from what I understand, we have a lot to do in a very short period of time." She consulted the tablet in her hand. Tapped the screen. "I've added to your calendar a meeting with John Marksman and Mr. Brunson for Friday morning, and our flight has been confirmed for seven on Monday," she said.

Powell drummed his fingers on the desk. "And Marksman, who is he?"

"I'm not sure. I couldn't find him in the directory." She swiped left and right on the tablet, as if double checking the directory.

"Come in, sit down," Powell said. He indicated the one chair in front of his desk. She sat. "Have you ever been to Africa?"

"No, sir."

"Louis, please. Not sir."

She pursed her lips, and nodded. "Aside from visiting Niagara Falls a few times, I haven't really been anywhere."

Wonderful. "I see," he said. "And this meeting on Friday?"

"Mr. Brunson's secretary set it up. Oh, and it's not here."

"It's not?"

"No. We'll be meeting them offsite."

"Offsite, where?" Powell said.

"Well, I looked into it," she said. She moved the chair closer to the desk. "It's an abandoned warehouse. Small building. It's on Steubenville Pike." She repeated the address.

"Are you kidding me? We're meeting at some abandoned warehouse?" He stood up. "I don't get it. Nothing about this day."

"You want me to reschedule?" She held fingers poised over the tablet.

Louis ran his hands through his hair. "No. No. I just wish I knew what was going on."

"I've got directions included in the event. We can drive over together if you like?"

"That will be fine," Powel said.

"If that's all, I'd like to head home and start packing," she said. "And according to Mr. Brunson, you do not need to report to work the rest of the week."

"I don't, huh?"

"No, sir."

"Louis. We agreed you'd call me Louis."

"Might take some getting used to," she said.

"I'll keep reminding you."

# # #

Louis spent the week getting things in order for a trip he didn't want to take. The idea of leaving the country for three months made him apprehensive. His banked online, so that wasn't an issue. He stopped his mail. The neighbor agreed to keep an eye on the house, and would check for mail that still got delivered. The kid down the street was going to take care of the lawn. He paid up front, and told him if it needs more attention to give it, and he'd make up the difference when he got home.

He picked his assistant up at the office. They drove to the warehouse in his Jeep. Claire fed him directions. They reached the warehouse in twenty minutes.

There were two vehicles parked on the side of the small building.

"Abandoned, huh?" Powell said.

"That's the information I found. And judging by the look of the place, I was right."

They stepped out of the Jeep. "Can I ask you something? You think this is on the up and up? I mean, I'm not doing anything illegal. I refuse to."

"I'm with you. I'm not breaking laws."

"Did you have to sign a bunch of papers with legal? Did you read them all? No? Me either," he said. "Do we just go in?" Powell said.

The sun rose in a blue and cloudless sky. The street was mostly empty.

Claire looked up and down the street. "I don't see why not."

Louis Powell was not comfortable.

"Well?" she said.

"Let's get this meeting started," Powell said. The raise should have been the first red flag. This warehouse, the second. Definitely a second.

A wire milk crate propped open a door on the west side of the building. Louis pulled the door open. He stuck his head inside. "Hello?"

"Mr. Powell. Ms. Askew. Please, come in."

It wasn't Gary Brunson doing the inviting. This man was tall, dressed in a black t-shirt, black pants, black boots. His hair was shaved off. His scalp polished to a shine. Powell's apprehension only grew, but walked into the warehouse, anyway.

The warehouse was one big grey room. Except for some tables in the center of the place, and some safes along the back wall, there was little else. The floors were simple cement. Light fixtures with fluorescent bulbs hung from the ceiling. Everything looked chipped, peeling, water damaged, or was a combination.

Although he'd only recently met Claire, he felt protective and wanted her more safely behind him. He wasn't much of a fighter. In high school, the few fights he'd been in, he'd lost. He couldn't remember ever landing a punch in any of the scraps. There was no reason for her to know that, though. "Anything seems funny, you run. Got it?" She said, "You don't have to tell me twice."

A door opened in the far right corner. Powell hadn't seen it at first. Had to be an office. Gary Brunson stepped out, saw them and smiled. "We're just waiting on Mr. Marksman. We can sit over here until he arrives."

An eight foot party table sat in the center of the warehouse. Around it were six metal folding chairs.

They didn't wait long. With the outside door propped open the rev of an approaching motorcycle engine was heard. There was a moment of silence, and then a man filled the doorway. He wore all black. Removing sunglasses and setting them on his head, he carried his helmet in one hand as he strode across the floor. "Sorry I'm late," he said.

Powell noticed the gun on a shoulder holster, and a knife in a sheath strapped to his leg.

"You're fine. We just sat down," Brunson said. "Please, join us. This is Mr. Louis Powell."

"The geologist?" Marksman said, and held out his hand.

"Not really," Powell said, shaking the man's hand.

"And his assistant, Ms. Claire Askew," Brunson said.

They shook hands, as well. "I'm John Marksman. Nice to meet both of you."

"Likewise," Claire said.

Marksman sat down next to Brunson.

"John is going to be your guide in the jungle. He and his team will protect the parcel of land. They are well trained for these types of situations."

Powell held up a hand. "Ah, situations?"

"The jungle. The natives. You want to feel comfortable in the Congo. John's going to ensure everything goes smooth," Brunson said.

Powell wondered why legal wasn't at the meeting. He was tempted to ask. "And, if I may, what do you foresee as being rough, or rocky with the expedition?"

"Nothing," Marksman said. "I've spent years in the Congo. I know it better than any city I've ever lived in. I'm a precaution. Nothing more. You don't need to worry."

"I wasn't, until I was told there was nothing to worry about. When people say things like that, it's usually because, well, there's something to worry about." Powell raised his hands as if surrendering.

Brunson laughed. "This is not like that at all."

"How many people in your team?" Powell said, ignoring his boss' flippant response.

"Six, including me," Marksman said.

"Six." Powell shook his head. "And you'll all be armed?"

"To the teeth." Marksman smiled.

"Mr. Brunson, I want to speak frankly here."

"And you should," Brunson said.

"I'm not sure I am comfortable with this. If we need mercenaries protecting us, it makes me a bit apprehensive about, well, everything."

"They are *not* mercenaries." Brunson pursed his lips and leaned back. He folded his hands and lowered them onto his lap.

"They're not?" Powell said.

"Well. Yes, they are. But they work for me. They are employees of Circuitz, no different than you. They are loyal to the company. They are being very well compensated for their services. Marksman has been under my supervision for nearly ten years," Brunson said. He didn't appear happy, as if being called out on the truth ruined his mood. His left eye twitched more than once while he spoke.

Powell wasn't impressed. Lying was not becoming on anyone, least of all his employer. Circuitz was asking for a lot from him. Was asking for the truth too much? It made him consider walking away. He appreciated his position with the company. The fact the boss was messing with his stability was unsettling.

"I assure you, both of you will be safe with my team. We're highly trained, and the best at what we do," Marksman said.

"The job is for three months. Would you feel better going into the rain forest alone?" Brunson said. It sounded like a threat.

"I just am not sure what to think. One, I'm hardly a geologist. Two, the coltan you showed me in the conference room the other day was the first time I'd ever seen the stuff. I'm hardly an expert, or qualified for this mission," Powell said. He wasn't playing a game. His degree was from a quality school. The job market might suck, but with his experience and education behind him, he was confident he'd find another job if it came down to it. The thing was, he was vested. Each year after that milestone made it harder to walk away.

"You are an exemplary employee. You manage a group of employees with the finesse and experience I've been looking for. I chose you as project manager because I believe you can go to the Congo and do the job that needs getting done. It's three months. Ninety days. I will include an additional bonus for both you and Ms. Askew," Brunson said, and told them an amount.

It was a lot of money. On top of the raise, it made walking away from the job almost impossible. Three months was tolerable, or more tolerable for the financial benefits they'd gain. "Seriously?"

"I never joke about money. Do we have a deal?" Brunson furrowed his brow. Powell knew his boss was serious, and wanted an answer.

Powell looked over at Claire. He cocked his head to the side, as if asking what she thought. Silently, she stared at him. He had the distinct feeling whatever he said, she'd go along with. He considered that. His decision affected her as well.

"Mr. Powell, I need an answer. Otherwise, I've wasted a lot of time. Other candidates will have to be interviewed." Mr. Brunson stood up.

Powell nodded. "Okay. Alright. Three months. I'm in."

"And Ms. Askew?" Brunson said.

"Me, too. I'm in," she said.

Brunson sat down. "Very well. I will have legal send you documents, and have the bonus payable upon your return. If we're done wasting time, John, why don't you take it from here."

"Key things. If you haven't already, I strongly suggest purchasing a quality pair of waterproof hiking boots. Light, waterproof trousers. You will tuck those into your boots and tie the laces tight." John stood up and put a booted foot on the chair. "Like this. With your pants tucked into your boot, nothing can get into your clothing."

Claire held up a hand.

"You don't have to do that," Marksman said. "What?"

"What don't I want getting up my pant leg?"

"The vegetation is very dense, thick. Sometimes the only way through is getting on the ground and crawling, or pulling yourself. You will want your sleeves taped off at the wrists, and pants tucked into your boots. Otherwise you invite in spiders, snakes, fire ants, mosquitoes and that kind of thing," he said.

She frowned. "Gotcha."

"Gloves are a good idea. These will protect you from sharp branches, stinging plants, and the dampness. You will want to pack toiletries and medical supplies. We will have antihistamines for stings, and antiseptic for scratches, but you will want things like razors, and shaving cream. Wet wipes for ... freshness. If you have any questions while you are out shopping, here is my card. Don't hesitate calling me. Otherwise, I will see you at the airport on Monday morning," Marksman said, handing out business cards.

CHAPTER 4

Powell was not a fan of flying. The idea of sitting in a machine and soaring over the Atlantic Ocean made him apprehensive. Just being in the air for twenty hours was challenging enough. The Boeing was luxurious enough, however. With minimal turbulence, the flight wasn't half bad. He'd tried sleeping, listening to music, and watching movies. Nothing removed the edge, until he started downing drinks. Claire Askew had no trouble sleeping. She used a postage stamp sized pillow, and reclined her seat two and a half inches and was out cold as soon as they were in the air.

The tough part about consuming alcohol on the trip was his constant need for relieving himself. Seatbelted into a chair on a plane felt safer than walking the narrow aisles to use the restroom every hour. It didn't slow down his drinking, though. The buzz he maintained kept him calmer than expected. Each time he stood and made his way to the bathroom, John Marksman eyed him.

This made Powell self conscious, as if his manhood was being called into question because of his small bladder.

When they landed in Uganda, he thought the worst leg of the trip was behind him, and he wouldn't need to worry about being up in the air again for ninety days. He figured going home would make the flight better just because they were going home.

In the small airport John Marksman secured a Rover. They loaded the backpacks and luggage in back. When they'd stepped off the plane the first thing Powell noticed was the stifling weight of humidity. Moisture appeared suspended in mid-air, and looked like it could be parted with the wave of a hand. It was as if thin, clear clouds surrounded them. It had either just rained, or was about to rain. Marksman didn't waste time. They purchased some food at one of the airport stands, and ate on the road.

Road was a rudimentary word. It suggested pavement, and street signs; yellow lines and traffic lights. The uneven dirt was red, and more like clay. They were bounced and banged around for hours. Powell couldn't be sure, but thought his thighs might be bruised.

The A/C worked well enough. The cold air shot out of the vents. It provided an illusion. Claire and Marksman chatted most of the drive. Powell sat in back and just stared out the fogged up window, wiping a palm across the glass every few minutes. For several miles, they passed villages with small hut-homes. Used American cars were parked here and there, and many of the people wore championship shirts of NFL teams who actually lost the Super Bowl. After crossing the border into the Democratic Republic of the Congo the land they passed became all the more breathtaking. Green mountains and plush forests lined both sides of the road. There were fewer villages, less cars, and he hadn't seen another human for miles.

"When we reach the boat launch, we'll have time for a quick dinner with the locals, and then we'll want to get on the Ulindi, and try to make it to camp by morning," Marksman said. "Early afternoon at the latest."

Powell was exhausted. He regretted not being able to sleep on the long flight. There was no way he could have slept on the drive. The idea of cruising along a river in the

Congo didn't sound any more promising. The sooner they reached camp, the better. That might be the first chance he'd get for sleeping.

An hour later, John Marksman parked the Rover outside of a long, rectangular tin-hut. "Food here is pretty good. Don't drink the water. Get something that comes in a bottle. Unopened," he said, shutting off the engine.

A man sat on a stack of discarded automobile tires smoking a cigarette staring at them. He held the cigarette below the knuckles between his fingers, and took a drag with his fingers erect and palm to his face. He wore jean shorts and a red Coke t-shirt.

"Plenty of hands will be held out. They see you're American. They assume you're rich. Well, to them, you are. You're Donald Fuckin Trump in their eyes. But listen to me, you don't give them anything. This country is one big humanitarian fucking disaster. The UN patrols the DROC, but they don't do a thing to help these people. Thing is, it's not our job to fix anything. What's best is if we just keep our eyes looking straight ahead, and get where we're going. You understand?" Marksman removed his gun from the shoulder holster and verified the clip was loaded.

"DROC?" Powell said.

"Democratic Republic of the Congo, DROC." He motioned with his head. "Let's go eat and get out of here."

They walked past the man on the tires and into an almost pitch black room. It took a while for Powell's eyes to adjust. Marksman led the way. Claire was sandwiched between them. People sat at tables inside. Marksman picked an empty one in a back corner. It was just a picnic bench. Something you'd see at a park, only with a white cloth sheet over the table. It was dirty. Powell wondered how often they were removed and washed.

Marksman sat with his back to the wall. He translated the French menu for Powell and Claire Askew. It was a sheet of loose-leaf paper stuffed into a plastic sleeve. There were three main items: Pan fried fish, whatever the catch of the day happened to be, with cooked plantains; Fufu, a sticky dough-like dish made of cassava flour; and goat meat with rice and vegetables. Any item ordered came with a side of pili pili. Marksman explained these were extremely hot peppers.

Powell watched Marksman. His eyes constantly scanned the room. He didn't even look the waitress in the eye when ordering. They all got the fish. Catfish was the catch of the day.

A man approached the table. A pipe dangled between bent forward yellow teeth. Puffs of smoke blew out of his mouth, and rose from the packed tobacco. His sky blue dress shirt was only partly tucked in, while a front flap hung out. The bottom few buttons were fastened. The rest left undone, revealing sweaty dark skin with aged scars across his chest. He spoke, his words lyrical sounding. Very French, Powell assumed.

Marksman smiled, but looked annoyed. He answered the man. His French appeared fluent and flawless.

Powell and Claire exchanged looks, mildly amused.

The man nodded toward them, and held out a hand. "Pin-twa" is what it sound like he said.

Powell shook his hand, and patted himself. "Louis."

Claire introduced herself.

Pin-twa sat down at the table across from them. He rested his elbows on his knees. Smoke filled the space around his head. Powell was reminded of a locomotive engine. One of the trains from the old west. The smoke pipe spitting plumes into the air as the wheels fought for traction on the rails. He couldn't help but imagine a whistle blowing.

The man continued talking with Marksman, and for the most part, Marksman responded. Until the food came. The man still wanted conversation. Marksman waved the man away. His tone of voice changed drastically.

Tension filled the diner. Powell casually looked around. Everyone was watching them, paying attention to the exchange. The waitress set the food in front of them and walked quickly away.

Pin-twa couldn't weigh more than a hundred and forty pounds, and was maybe five-eight. Marksman was armed to the teeth with knives and guns. It wouldn't be much of a fight. Powell assumed Marksman wouldn't need a weapon. Marksman was muscular, the soaked in sweat black t-shirt he wore clung to pecs and biceps and six pack abs as if the cotton was painted onto his skin.

Pin-twa tried again, as if what he needed to say was vital. His eyes were open wide. He held the pipe away from his mouth, as he stood up and pleaded.

Marksman jumped to his feet. He slammed a hand on the table. While he responded in French, he waved at the food, and pointed at Powell and Claire. He climbed over the bench he sat on and made an aggressive step toward Pin-twa.

Pin-twa held his ground. He pointed in general toward front of the diner.

The two stood toe-to-toe.

Neither said a word.

Pin-twa shook his head, and his shoulder slouched. He looked at Powell and said in English. "I am sorry. I tried. Be careful."

He walked to the exit and left the diner.

Marksman stayed standing and stared the rest of the patrons down before sitting in front of his meal.

"Um," Claire said. "What just happened?"

Marksman shook his head. He inspected the fork on his plate, and wiped it up and down on the table cloth. "Locals."

"We got that," Powell said. "What was he saying?"

"What was he sorry about?"

Marksman forked his food around on the plate. Set the fork down and sighed. "The guy knows why we're here. Word gets around. I hate that. We don't need our operation publicly displayed. We're going to be out in the jungle, okay? The less people that know, the better."

"The less people that know? That doesn't sound safe," Powell said.

"It is. Trust me," Marksman said. He leaned forward and whispered, "Coltan is bread and butter for a lot of people here. Some would just as soon steal the mineral after it's been mined, rather than get their hands dirty."

"And that's what he was warning us about? Raiders?" Claire said.

"No. Not exactly. It was nonsense. That's all. Nonsense." Marksman stabbed his fish. The fried breading crumbled, exposed white meat. He ate some. Chewed it. Swallowed. Set his fork down. His elbows were on the table. His hands folded together. "Look, we aren't back home. This ain't Kansas anymore, if you know what I'm saying?"

"I don't know what you're saying," Powell said. "What are you saying? Because a Wizard of Oz reference seems appropriate, but I am too tired for riddles."

Marksman let himself smile. He moved the food around on his plate some more. Ate another bite of fish. "Eat. Don't let the fish get cold."

"The humidity will keep it warm," Claire said. "Please, continue."

"The locals spread around this rumor." Marksman set down his fork and ran his tongue over his teeth. "The nice gentleman who I was just talking with wanted to make sure we were aware of. . ."

When Marksman stopped talking, Powell said, "Aware of what?"

"The Kasai Rex," he said.

"The what? What is that?"

"It's a fabled dinosaur. They call it the Elephant Killer."

"A dinosaur," Powell said.

"Never went extinct. Survived the Ice Age, or meteor showers sixty million years ago and is alive and well living in the Congo," Marksman said. He stared at them, waiting.

Claire laughed first.

Then Powell.

"They think there's a dinosaur in the jungle?" Claire said.

"A giant dinosaur. Bigger than the, what is it? From that movie. . . Tyrannosaurus Rex. The T-Rex." Marksman smiled. "Told you it was ludicrous."

"Something like that, we'd have seen it? YouTube or Facebook or something." Powell ate some of the catfish, raised an eyebrow in surprise at the wonderful flavor.

"Thing is," Marksman said.

Powell stopped chewing.

"A lot of people are going missing in the jungle. Don't get all crazy. It's not a K-Rex. We're not idiots. Safety is key. That's why I'm here. As long as you do what I say, when I say, without question, my team and I will be able to protect you, protect Circuitz investment, and we'll all make a little money while we're at it. *Capisce*?"

Marksman was not Italian. *Capisce* sounded funny coming out of his mouth. "Got it," Powell said. He laughed again, lifting flaky fish to his mouth. "A dinosaur. Too funny.

# # #

Louis Powell missed the uneven and bumpy road. He longed for the air-conditioned SUV. The jungle was dense. Green, plush, and dense. He never would have thought to pack gloves. He'd thank Marksman when they eventually stopped walking. Swinging the machete to cut a path on the path was exhausting. He still figured his palms would blister.

They hacked at giant leaves, tall stalks and low-hanging branches. If he wasn't so out of breath from hiking in the heat and humidity, he would complain. Complaining wouldn't get him anything. It was obvious why they couldn't get the Rover through the thicket of the forest. Walking was challenge enough.

Using his forearm, Powell continually swiped at sweat on his brow, keeping the salty beads out of his eyes. He took big steps. The last thing he wanted was tripping, falling, and winding up injured. He also did not want to accidently step on anything. When he set his foot down, half his leg was lost to growth on the ground.

Things in the jungle squawked and chirped, buzzed and squealed. It was both surreal and amazing. He thought of it like the first time he'd seen the ocean. Standing on a sandy beach in Florida, he stared out at the water, watching the waves crash onto the shore and realized just how insignificant he truly was. It was like that now. The canopy above him, the animals and insects around him were overwhelming.

"Forgot to mention it, but if we come across gorillas," Marksman shouted over his shoulder. "We're in trouble."

Powell swung the machete. The stalk toppled. It looked like a dirt path for the next few yards. The easy life. "That's funny," he said.

Marksman stopped walking. He removed a canteen off his belt. "It's not funny. The gorillas are not friendly. They will kill us before we can get twenty feet."

Powell watched the merc drink water. "Do they live in these parts?"

"These parts? If you mean the Congo, then yes. They live in these parts. Have a sip of water. Catch your breath, and we'll get started again," Marksman said.

"We getting close? I feel like we've been walking for three hours." Claire twisted the cap off her bottle, but before taking a drink she removed her hat and poured some of her water onto the top of her head.

"Don't waste that water," Marksman said.

"I'm hot."

"We've been walking for less than two hours. We will continue until it is dark, and then find a place to make camp for the night. By this time tomorrow, we should reach the Circuitz parcel, where my team and the company employees will be hard at work. So if you have twenty-four hours of water in your canteen, have at it. Take a bath if you want. Me, I'm saving mine. Drinking it in small sips like this." He demonstrated taking a small sip of his water. He replaced the cap and clipped the canteen back onto his belt. "Let's keep moving."

"We're going to sleep in the jungle?" Claire said, whispering.

Powell tried smiling. For some reason, he envisioned a building beside the dig site on the parcel. Worse case, a small hut. He suddenly wasn't as confident about the idea of a structure existing. He now imagined tents. Muddy, bug-infested tents. "Only for the next three months, Ms. Askew. Only for the next three months."

CHAPTER 5

"Sir, we were starting to think a search party was going to be needed." The woman stepped out from between trees. Powell had not seen her prior to. She was clearly a female version of John Marksman. Dressed in black cargo pants, the legs tucked into tightly laced black boots, and heavily armed, she smiled as she said hello. She wore an Ares-16 Assault Rifle strapped over her shoulder. A large knife in a sheath was strapped against each thigh. The black tank-top she had on was mostly hidden under a heavy Kevlar vest that had anti-tank and stun grenades, as well as extra ammo clips affixed to it.

Powell wondered why he hadn't been allowed to say the word mercenary. There was no denying this was a paramilitary outfit.

"Jennings! We found such a perfect place to hole up for the night, we overslept this morning. Got off to a bit of a late start," Marksman said. He made introductions. "Follow me. We'll get you set up, and then I'll show you around and introduce you to the other members of my team."

"How many others are there?" Claire asked.

"There's Stacy Jennings, who you just met, and four others."

Powell wondered where the mining operation was. They were still in the midst of a jungle. The canopy blocked sunlight, and if it was raining, he couldn't tell. It seemed like water dripped off leaves overhead nonstop since they started on the way that morning.

He walked, following behind Claire and Marksman. Stacy Jennings remained where she was, a perimeter post he assumed. His legs were like jelly. His workouts at the gym every other day hadn't prepared his body for this kind of exertion. Worse, the boots he'd purchased kept his feet protected from everything, but because they were new, tore up his feet. He knew he'd need band aids, or ointments. He left them on last night. He worried about what might happen when he took them off. Would his feet swell up?

He looked at Claire's feet.

She wore brand new boots, as well. Figuring she couldn't be any better off, he kept his mouth shut. She hadn't complained about the conditions once. He hadn't either, but the temptation was there. He was here because of money. Enough had been set in front of him by Brunson that he couldn't afford to walk away.

And yet, now he wondered if any of this was worth a raise?

Three months. Ninety days. He could do this. He'd have stories worth telling in bars. "Back when I was in the Congo..."

He smiled.

Missing the simple things from home already gnawed at him. Shitting in the woods was crazy. He'd held it as long as he could. When they made camp for the night, he continued holding it. He wasn't venturing off in the dark. He supposed if Claire hadn't been there, he'd have had no issue with the act. First thing that morning, he practically had to run between trees while pulling his pants down. He didn't like the vulnerable exposure. His junk wasn't much, but it worked and it was his. Having it dangle out in the open was uncomfortable. It wasn't snakes and spiders worrying him.

He didn't want his pecker bit by a huge mosquito. And the thing he feared most was contracting malaria from an insect sucking blood out of his dick. He'd pooped as fast as possible and hoped things would be more modern once they made it to camp.

They reached a clearing. Trees and stumps were cleared away from a sizeable piece of land. Had to be at least 175 sq. feet. There was a backhoe parked on one side, and a flat dirt road led into the parcel, a ramp for driving in and out. The earth was dug up pretty good. It reminded Powell of a gravel pit. It wasn't as deep, maybe only from six to ten feet down, or so. The depth progressed from one end to the other like an in-ground swimming pool.

Their home and place of work for the next three months was a hundred times better than Powell anticipated. It still looked rough, and third-world, but there were four walls and a makeshift roof. "This isn't too bad."

Marksman pointed to the *building*. "It's mud and stick walls. Requires extra attention. We worked with the Congolese, tying strips of bamboo to the support poles of the wall. Making mud isn't an issue. It rains all the freaking time. We press it into mud balls and put them in between the slotted bamboo walls, which lends to the solid look of the place. The roof is just layer and layer of palm fronds. There is no electricity, no running water, and the latrine is a small hut behind this one. Heavy rain or storms, and we're holed up inside like the three little pigs, if you know what I mean?"

Powell changed his mind. The place was awful. He could not imagine sleeping in a place with mud for walls. "It doesn't look like mud and sticks and bamboo," he said.

Marksman laughed and clapped him on the back. "It's wood, son. Wood, and a tin roof. We still slapped the palm fronds on top though, over the tin. It helps with noise reduction. Rain pinging on a tin roof all night, and none of us would get any rest."

Powell exhaled a sigh of relief. "Seriously? That's great. I'm so relieved to hear it. I can't even tell ya. You had me worried there. Okay, so there's a bathroom inside then?"

Marksman's smile vanished, and he shook his head. "Nope. Latrine is out back. No kitchen either. We cook outside. Tried it once or twice when the weather was bad. Place fills with smoke too fast. Can't even breathe. Could have cut a hole in the roof for ventilation, but I'd rather cook outside than have a hole in the roof."

# # #

Introductions with the remainder of Marksman team went quick. Powell felt like he was on a Black Ops mission in some Tom Clancy film. Only thing missing on the mercenaries was the black and green makeup stripes painted on their faces. They were each Marksman's mirrored image. Muscle, dressed in black, and heavily armed.

They were all inside the cabin—how Marksman referred to the dwelling—eight cots lined the walls. There were three tables with chairs in the center, and a bookcase with books and board games against the back wall. Crude and rudimentary. There was no privacy. No walls. It was just one big open floor plan, but there was a floor. Plywood. It was better than plain earth. There were large rectangular windows. Powell walked up to one and tapped on it with a knuckle. Plexiglass.

Marksman had his team standing and lined up behind him. Powell and Claire sat at the first table, across from one another.

"You met Stacy outside," John Marksman said. She nodded a second, silent, hello. He moved on to the next person in line, standing at attention. "This is Ian Ross. He's from England. Say hello, Ian."

"'Ello."

Marksman laughed. "Love that accent. Ian was with the United Kingdom Special Forces, and involved with counterterrorism, unconventional warfare, as well as special and covert reconnaissance missions. Took some shrapnel in the thigh during a mission that went wrong and was released to early medical retirement. Anyone want to see the scar on his leg? No? Okay then.

"This here is Rebecca Robinson. Becky. Like Stacy and I, she was a U.S. Marine. The three of us were deployed on countless Black Ops missions. We've performed clandestine search and rescue missions in Afghanistan, Iran, Iraq, and Vietnam. We each served consecutive tours, and for our own personal reasons decided not to re-up any longer," Marksman said. "Becky, say hello."

"Hello," she said.

"No accent. Still as cute as Ian, if you ask me," he said.

Powell wondered if the marines made connections during their service, and realized the money was there to be made for doing the same job, just for an employer other than the United States of America? He didn't ask, because he did not feel the question would be well received.

The next man was black. His skin was nearly as dark as his clothing. "Charlie Erb," Marksman said. "He comes to us from the Special Operations Command from down under. He's been assigned to task groups involved with the world's global fight against terrorism. He's spent nearly five years in

Afghanistan, and a few years in places he won't reveal even to us. Files are sealed up tight, too. So I just take him at his word when he tells me the confidential assignments were dangerous. Isn't that right, Charlie?"

"That's right," Erb said.

"Say hello to our colleagues from Circuitz," Marksman said, and Erb did. "Last, but certainly not least, is Jack Shelton. He was an NYPD sergeant, and a member of the elite Special Weapons and Tactics unit, or S.W.A.T. Knowing this man was born, raised and served his twenty years in the Big Apple, you might think he is out of place in the rain forest? You'd be wrong. The man belongs in the jungle. Right at home in the Congo, aren't ya, Shelton?"

"It's home," he said.

"Hear that? Home," Marksman said. "Any questions anyone?"

Powell felt like he should raise his hand. He refrained. "We're not the first two...corporate types sent to this location from Circuitz, are we?"

Marksman shook his head. "You are not the first project manager, no."

"How long has this dig been going on?"

"Nearly five years," Marksman said. He stood with his hands laced together behind his back, feet shoulder width apart.

"So what happened to the others?" Powell couldn't recall anyone he worked with leaving for the Congo, nor even hearing about anyone from the corporation going.

"They spend their three months here and leave. Same as you." Marksman shifted his weight, and brought his hands around. "Just a few rules. Use the latrine before bed. There's no going out in the middle of the night. If you absolutely can't hold it until morning, wake me. You make a mess, you clean it up. We aren't servants, we're a security detail. We do the cooking, however. Fish from the nearby river, meat from whatever we kill. There is no menu. You want something different to eat, catch it, kill it, and cook it yourself. There are no left overs. Ever. Whatever isn't consumed is removed from our area. We don't want animals sniffing around at night looking for food. It's dangerous enough when they are nearby out of curiosity. However you manage the locals for the dig is up to you. We won't interfere. On the site, you call the shots. So far we've had minimal issues with the natives. They show up each morning to work, and they leave an hour or two before dusk. They walk to and from, and don't want to be in the forest at night either. If you have an employee giving you problems, see anyone of us. We'll get it straightened out. It's best if you don't get involved with any discipline. Other than that, I think we've covered everything. Any questions?"

Claire raised her hand.

"You don't need to do that. This isn't school," Marksman said. "What?"

"What about showers?"

"There aren't any. Every couple of days, we'll head down to the river to bathe. That's another thing you don't want to do alone. It's not just what might be in the water that makes it dangerous. We clear?"

Stacy said, "A good rain works, too. Stand out in it and wash. Modesty will only leave you smelling rancid and raw. If you stink too badly, we'll strip you ourselves and scrub you. We've only had to do it once before. Once."

Claire's smile resembled more of a grimace. "Got it," she said.

CHAPTER 6

Breakfast consisted of nuts, fruits and vegetables. Coffee was brewed on a pan over an open fire. Powell slept like shit. The mattress on the cot was two inches thick. Tossing and turning made up most of the night. Sitting in the latrine, since the coffee was strong and like an instant enema, he tried looking on the bright side: eighty-nine days to go.

He'd brought his cell phone, along with five battery packs. There were no outlets. He left it in his bag under his cot. The idea of being cut off from the rest of the world for a quarter of the year made him apprehensive. He already missed the stupid things like Facebook and Twitter, email and Instagram. He tried thinking this could be a good thing. The cell phone dictated his life. Here was an opportunity to regain control.

Claire was by the dig. She somehow looked fresh and ready for the day.

"How'd you sleep?" he said, standing next to her.

"Would have been good, if someone didn't toss and turn the whole time," she said.

"You mean *me*?"

"Why? Was someone *else* restless last night?" She laughed.

People walked toward them. The well-worn path was still covered in overgrown everything. They carried cloth bags with knots tying them off at the top. "Those must be the miners?"

"You ever done this before?"

"Mined for coltan? No. I searched it on the internet. It's done the same way we dug for gold back during the gold rush," he said.

"Yeah, I wasn't alive then," she said. "I looked it up as well. I read the descriptions, watched some videos. Doesn't seem too difficult. Looks like we're just actually digging here. Chipping away at the earth piece by piece. Pulling out the hunks found."

"Easy, right?" Powell counted three males and two females. Best guess, not one of them was over twenty. One looked about she might be twelve, thirteen at the most. "They're kids."

"No labor laws here? It's kind of like a sweatshop, but outside?" Claire said.

"Better not be. I'm not going to mistreat these people," Powell said.

The mercenaries surrounded the pit perimeter. They looked vigilant with hands on the assault rifles, ready for the unexpected. They've been out here years. Maybe everything they were prepared for was now expected. He hoped so. Surprises could be cool, like for a birthday party or something. Out here in the Congo, he wasn't in the mood for surprises. Plain, ordinary, boring days would be ideal. Time might drag, but at least at the end of the stay he'd go home.

"Know what's crazy?"

"Tell me," she said.

"We've been gone a couple of days, and already all I can think about is grabbing a burger and fries."

"It's morning. You just woke up," she said.

"A sundae. Chocolate and vanilla ice cream, a sliced-up banana, and hot fudge."

"Now you have my attention."

More people came down the path. They smiled walking by Powell and Claire. They each set their cloth wrapped belongings down beside a tree, and then walked down the dirt road into the pit. Below, they retrieved pickaxes and shovels, and began hacking away at the ground.

"I don't know what we're supposed to be doing here, not really," Powell said.

"Aren't you a geologist?"

He laughed. "No. I minored in geology in college."

"Minored?"

"That's it." Held both hands up, as if admitting guilt. "What about you? How did you get to be my assistant?"

Claire said, "My boss retired last year. They've been farming me out to different departments like a temp. Cindy was on maternity. Gloria had that gastric bypass surgery. Wherever there was an opening, I was sent to fill it. Hated that. When they brought this up to me as a three month assignment, I jumped on it. And, the best part, they promised a permanent spot when I return."

"Not a bad deal, then," Powell said. "I suggest we head into the pit, introduce ourselves."

"Good call, boss. I agree."

They walked toward the dirt road by the backhoe. "Have you ever seen coltan?"

"I haven't."

"Me either. I suppose we should give mining for it a shot. See what the job is like. That make sense?" he suggested. It was going to be a humid day. When it rained, and from what he'd learned about the Congo it rained a lot, the pit must be like a gigantic swimming pool filled with mud.

"Mining might be a great way to pass the time. And, since I'm not a member at any of the local gyms, I welcome the chance to exercise," she said, smiling.

Ian Ross nodded a hello. "Going into the pit?"

"We thought we'd introduce ourselves. Give mining a shot. Check things out."

"Good deal. Good deal. You speak their language?" Ian said.

"French? No. They all speak French?" Powell hadn't given much thought to a language barrier before this moment. He supposed he knew it existed, but hadn't thought about how they'd all communicate without Marksman around for interpretation purposes.

"Them? I have no idea what they speak. Sometimes it sounds like French, other times it just comes off like gibberish." Ian didn't sound cruel when he slammed the native language. It was more like he was doing his best at explaining what was what.

Powell noticed an earpiece in Ian's ear. "Can you hear and talk to the others on your team from here, Mr. Ross?"

Ian frowned. "Don't Mr. Ross me. You do that, and you're going to make me feel like I have to call you Mister-whatever-your-last-name was, or boss, or sir, and guess what? I don't do that shit no more. I'm Ian. Ian is what you call me."

"Fine. Sure. I'm Louis."

"Louis, I remember. And Claire," Ian said.

"The earpiece, you guys are all connected?" Powell said, pointing at the white coil that led from his shirt collar up to his ear.

"Of course. We are in constant communication with each other," he said.

"How do you charge the equipment? I thought there wasn't electricity out here?" Powell said.

"There isn't electricity. In the hut behind the cabin, there's a small generator room. We keep industrial batteries in there," Ian said.

"Like for cell phones?"

"Not for cell phones," Ian said, "but yeah. Cell phones."

Powell grinned. He knew he had to look idiotic. He wanted to connect his phone now. Was already anxious to use it. Burgers. Fries. Facebook. How was he going to make it in the jungle for three months? He hoped Claire and Ian didn't recognize his anxiety. He needed to play it cool. "Marksman didn't mention that on our one room tour. He must have forgotten. Good though. That's good to know."

# # #

Powell felt immediately uncomfortable once down in the pit. The ground was soft. His boots sank a little after each step. Those mining chanced a look over their shoulder at him, apparently curious. He did his best at smiling and waving hello. He wanted to look friendly. He figured he just looked out of place.

They stopped by a large man with a pickaxe. Claire kept her hands folded in front of her.

The man eyed them.

Powell pressed his hand to his chest, as if about to recite the Pledge of Allegiance. "Louis." Claire did the same, and said her name: "Claire."

The man stared at them.

Powell tried it again with his name, and then touched his assistant on the shoulder. "Claire."

"Akia," the man said.

Powell had no idea what to say next. He held out his hand."It is nice to meet you."

Akia shook Powell's hand, and then slowly turned around, and when he was sure Powell and Claire had walked past him, swung the pickaxe.

"I think we're done introducing ourselves," Powell said. He saw the two young ladies working side by side. They used twelve-inch-long hand picks and stood by the dirt wall and chipped away at it, burrowing little holes here and there. "I don't think I like little kids working here, like this."

"You going to fire them, then? Give them a final day's pay and send them home?" Claire said. "I've looked over the books. They're making good money. Not just for the Congo, but for the U.S. Brunson's not being cheap."

"I can't fire them. But I want to make sure they get plenty of breaks and whatever else they need," Powell said. "Who do I see to make sure that happens?"

Claire arched eyebrows and cocked a hip. "Are you joking right now?"

"Joking?"

"You're the foreman. This is your dig for the next three months," she said.

"I'm the project manager." And then it hit him. "I'm the foreman. I am in charge."

"You are in charge," she said.

He shook his head. He didn't know what he'd gotten himself into, so he lied. "I knew that."

"Mr. Geology, can you show me what coltan looks like?"

"On your break. Right now, grab a pick and start whacking," he said.

"And what are you going to do?"

He smiled. "Grab a pick and join you. You know? This isn't too terrible. I'm kind of excited about finding some coltan. It's not gold. "

"So I'm learning," she said. "So I'm learning."

CHAPTER 7

At midday, the thunder roared from the hills above them and echoed through the valleys. The dark clouds rolled across the sky. The blanket of charcoal-grey covered the sunlight. The lightning flashed like blue sparks bouncing around inside the clouds as if part of a Tesla system. The rain came down fast and hard. It felt wonderful. Powell relished the relief. His clothing had been sticking to his skin, drenched with sweat and covered in dirt.

The problem was the pit floor. It became one large puddle. The lightning strikes shot down from the clouds. The storm was directly over them. Somewhere close a tree must have been hit. The sound was loud, a crack and boom. The tall trees were an easier target. Nothing prevented the lightning from hitting one of them.

"This isn't safe," Powell said. He was yelling. Claire nodded. "Everyone, out of the pit. Out."

No one moved. They all stopped digging and stared at him.

He waved his arm for the others to follow. Walking was difficult. Every step he took, he worried the mud would suck his boot off his foot. It reminded him of a reoccurring nightmare he had. In the dream, something was after him. The ground turned to something like glue, or molasses. As hard as he tried to run away from the unseen danger, he never made it anywhere.

Looking back he saw everyone else also struggling in the mud.

"The backhoe," Claire said, pointing.

Powell wasn't interested in the backhoe. Right now they needed to focus on finding safe shelter.

The younger girl was talking fast, upset. She looked scared. Her eyes were open wide. Her hands were against her face. The storm frightened her. Powell couldn't blame her. The storm scared him, too. They were standing in water. If lightning hit the shallow pool, they could be seriously hurt, or worse. He had to get everyone out of the water.

The slightly older girl tried picking up the one about to cry. The extra weight made it tougher for them to move. Powell credited the older one for making the effort.

Powell looked up and around the lip for the mercenaries. They waved for everyone to get out. They sounded encouraging. From above the pit, they weren't much help. There wasn't much more they could do. Coming down into the pit didn't make sense. Why risk their lives, too? That wouldn't solve the problem of getting out.

"I'm going to grab the girls. You get out of the pit. Now," Powell said.

"The others..."

"Claire, get out of the pit!"

Thunder exploded above them. Lingered. The lightning came next. It illuminated the clouds. It bounced around inside them, turned the grey clouds blue. Multiple bolts were hurled at the earth. A loud crack resounded. Somewhere, another tree had definitely been struck.

The ground, saturated, wasn't interested in the rain. The water was already an inch and a half deep. None of it was being absorbed into the dirt. Powell's legs felt too heavy. He leaned forward as the wind whipped around him. The thunder was steady. The lightning continuous. The rain pelted exposed skin, and surprisingly, stung.

People shouted behind him, a lot of yelling. He looked back. The miners were on the road, stopped. The bank the backhoe sat on caved. The dirt wall crumbled. The backhoe was about to topple. "Claire!"

She stood under the backhoe. Her legs were as stuck in the mud as his. She was having trouble getting out of the way.

Powell wanted to save her. He started toward her. He couldn't move fast. He tried, though. His legs strained against the mud. His muscles burned in his thighs. He fell forward when his right boot pulled free. He splashed into the thick sludge. It covered his clothing and face. His hands were coated in it. He tried wiping it out of his eyes.

When the last of the wall gave way, the backhoe fell into the pit. It came down in slow motion, as if it scrambled for a hold on the wall trying to keep itself from crashing into the earth. It toppled over onto its side. "Claire!"

It fell inches from her. "I'm okay!"

The lightning flashes lit the sky. Rolling thunder rumbled around them. The planet seemed to shake from the clamoring tumult. The intensity of the storm grew. The tall trees were bent. The howling wind was insistent.

Powell pushed himself up onto his feet. He trudged his way toward the young girls. When he reached them, they were both hugging each other, crying. Above him was Marksman. He was on his belly reaching down to them. Powell snatched up the smallest girl. She screamed.

"It's okay. It's okay," he said. He yelled, or else he would not be heard. That didn't help calming the children.

Why did he have children working for him?

The girl twisted in his grasp. He knew she was frightened, but she needed to relax. She obviously didn't understand

English. Nothing he said would soothe her. So instead of trying to calm her, he hoisted her in the air, well above his head. Marksman shouted orders, possibly in French. The child lifted her arm. Marksman latched on. He pulled her out of the pit.

"You're next," Powell said to the second girl. She was a little older, slightly taller. He laced his hands together and held them down. "Step into my hands. Step right there."

She stared at him.

He lifted his leg and showed her what to do, placing his cupped hands under his foot. "See? Step into my hands."

He held out his hands. He nodded encouragingly toward her. She was hesitant.

More lightning filled the dark sky. It reminded Powell of the beginning to some B-horror film, as if some mad scientist was in a lab attempting the reanimation of dead tissue. "Climb up, honey. Climb up."

She set her foot into his hands. Her hands went on his shoulders as he lifted her in the air. Her hands reached for Marksman. The toe of her other foot kicked into the mud wall. She helped climb her way out.

Powell looked around the pit. Everyone else was out. It was going to be a long trek across the pit.

The backhoe looked to be sinking. He didn't even want to think about that now. He had no idea how they got the monster piece of machinery here in the first place. He couldn't imagine anyway of towing it free. Brunson was not going to be happy.

Thunder clamored above.

Marksman yelled, "Take my hand!"

Powell looked up. Rain fell into his eyes. His vision blurred. Dirt and rainwater ran down his face. The heat and humidity didn't combat the chill he felt in his bones. He stretched up his arm. Marksman clasped onto his forearm and yanked. Powell used his legs and feet. He didn't have much more strength. His energy was drained. He climbed the muddy wall; it slid out from under his weight.

Once out of the pit, he wanted to collapse. There was no time. He needed to ensure everyone was okay.

"Are you okay?" Marksman said.

"What should we do?"

"Get everyone to the cabin until this passes."

They all made their way for the cabin, running close together.

"Claire, are you okay?" Powell said.

"I'm fine, I'm okay," she said.

They filled the cabin, everyone wet, and dirty. Everyone safe, and alive.

Akia was hollering something. He said it over and over. He kept pointing at the windows. Something else was wrong.

CHAPTER 8

The rain fell relentlessly. It hammered the cabin. The wind threatened to scatter the large leaves off the roof. They flapped above. The wind picked up speed. It screamed and whistled as it crashed through trees and branches. The storm loomed above them. Thankfully, the thunder was somewhat muffled inside the cabin. The lightning surrounded them, setting the outside aglow through the Plexiglass windows.

Akia's shadow was illuminated by each flash. He was by the window, pointing. He kept shouting something over and over. He wouldn't look away.

"What's he saying?" Powell said.

Claire stood beside him. She was shivering and filthy. She grabbed onto his arm.

"He said something was out there," Marksman said. He re-gripped his hold on the assault rifle. "It's nothing."

Powell looked around the room. "This isn't everyone. Where are the others?"

Claire said, "What do you mean it's nothing? It's something. Look at him. He's terrified."

"There were more than five people working in the pit," Powell said. He pointed at each person as he recounted. Eight mercenaries. Five employees. Himself, and Claire. "There were more than just fifteen of us."

Akia continued shouting. It was the same thing over and over.

"What did he see out there?" Claire said.

Marksman looked around at his team. "He thinks he saw a K-Rex."

"A K-Rex. The thing you told us was a myth," Claire said.

"It is a myth. The storm can do that. You have the wind blowing branches all over the place. It got dark fast. The lightning makes it look like a strobe light in some dance club. Everything gets distorted. You can't tell a person from a tree trunk," Marksman said. He turned toward Akia and spoke at him in a harsh tone of voice.

Akia held his hands together in front of him, his fingers fidgeted with one another. He lowered his head, as if ashamed. His eyes still darted toward the window, expectantly. Marksman pointed at one of the cots and barked a command. Akia was hesitant. He slowly moved away from the window. It looked like he was being dragged by an unseen force. Eventually he shuffled his way over and sat on a cot. He kept his hands laced together on his lap. His lips moved quickly, but no words escaped his mouth, as if he might be praying.

"Louis," Claire said. "Did you hear that? Something was out there. That K-Rex thing."

Powell held up a hand. He wasn't as concerned about a spooked native. He wasn't an idiot. There wasn't time to worry about imaginary monsters. He was in the middle of his own crisis. The backhoe toppled into the pit, and he had no idea how to excavate it. He didn't even know how they would upright it. He'd been on-site a full day and the operation was in serious jeopardy. Topping it off, and perhaps more of an immediate concern were the other, missing, employees. "Marksman? Ask what happened to the others that were working with us, please," he said.

"They run home. They're used to rain, but storms like this make them apprehensive, you know?" Marksman said.

"Make me feel better, ask them," Powell said. He could not imagine running through the dense forest during such a storm. Maybe the Congolese didn't understand how lightning worked and that hiding under trees during a storm was dangerous. "Marksman, please."

Marksman grunted. He spoke to the five workers. He paced the floor.

Powell watched their expressions. They watched John Marksman while he talked. One of the men said something and pointed.

"What did he say?" Powell said. He attempted introductions, patting his chest. "Powell."

"Ruhakana. Ruh," the young man said. He was shorter and far stockier than Akia. His skin was nearly as dark. His red and white striped dress shirt was covered in filth. His khaki shorts dripped. He stood barefoot in a puddle. If he was over fourteen years old, Powell would be shocked. The young man had a baby face look to him.

"Ruh. Nice to meet you," Powell said. "What did *Ruh* say?"

"He said he saw the others run into the trees, headed home," Marksman said in a cocksure tone of voice. He even stood cocky-like, as if saying, *See. I told you.*

"All of them, Ruh? All of them ran home?" Powell said. "Ask him, Marksman."

"Asked, and answered," Marksman said.

"Our people are out in that storm. They could get lost, or hurt. We won't know," Powell said.

"Are you suggesting we follow them to make sure they made it home?" Marksman said.

Ian Ross said something. Marksman held up a hand, silencing the member of his team. "Listen, Powell. This isn't like the states. I don't want to sound like a heartless asshole here, but we're not going out in the storm. You want to go look for them, be my guest. I hope nothing happened to the others. I do. I swear. But if they get hurt, that's not our problem. There's no workers' compensation here, if you know what I'm saying."

He was right. He did sound like a heartless asshole.

Powell pursed his lips. Marksman knew he couldn't go looking for the others. He wouldn't know what was or wasn't a path. He'd be lost in ten minutes. How would he track them? They could have exited the path at any point, and it was highly unlikely they all lived in the same area. Marksman assessment wasn't wrong; it was just his attitude that annoyed him.

"We better get comfortable. It could prove to be a long night," Powell said, addressing everyone.

Claire whispered, "What about what Akia said?"

"There's nothing out there, Claire. It's a storm," Powell said.

"Did you see his face, how scared that guy was? I believe him. I think he saw something."

"A dinosaur? Please, Claire. We have to figure out how to get that backhoe righted. If you want to worry about something useful, worry about that. We have to come up with an idea." Powell knew he'd lost his temper. He felt bad taking it out on Claire. He didn't have the time or patience for discussing prehistoric nonsense. There was no denying an overwhelming sense of dread in the jungle. He felt it, a little scared. Admitting this was another thing altogether. He wouldn't do that. The idea that a monster was just beyond the pit waiting to eat them, though, was ridiculous. If anything, he was more worried about spiders, snakes, gorillas, and lions. Those were viable threats.

CHAPTER 9

Once the storm passed, the workers seemed anxious about going home. Well, everyone except Akia. He hadn't moved off the cot. Powell was too tired for arguing, he instructed Marksman to tell everyone they could go home in the morning. When it was light out. They wouldn't be expected to work the next day. He wanted Marksman to assure them they would still be paid. No one would lose wages because of the storm.

"Their families will be worried about them," Marksman said.

"Tell them it's better they show up in the morning alive, than risk walking home in the dark and, God forbid, something happens to them," Powell said.

"Tell them that?" Marksman said.

"Yes. Tell them," Powell said. He knew he might sound a little overprotective. He didn't care about workers' compensation issues. He was concerned for these people. This might be their normal surroundings, and they might be comfortable with them, but he wasn't. They made him fretful. Way he saw it, he might never feel at ease in the jungle. It was a jungle, after all.

Powell barely slept. He sat on the floor, back to the wall after he'd given his cot to the two young girls. Too much was on his mind. It was a whirlwind of thoughts whipping about inside his brain. He didn't care if he lost his job. Getting fired was one of the least of his issues. It didn't stop that thought from taking up space in his skull. He didn't want to stay in the Congo for three months. Contract or not. He wanted to go home. It wasn't about being scared. It was more about wanting to get the fuck out the jungle. He couldn't believe he'd sold out. For a few extra dollars, he'd let Circuitz own him. Whose fault was that? Not theirs. The pennies they threw his way didn't impact their bottom line at all. They made billions each and every year. Giving him an extra five or ten thousand a year, what was that to them? It was nothing. Nothing. He let his personal greed get the best of him.

He didn't even like camping. The one time he went camping with his family, he'd hated it. His father rented a spot at the amusement park campgrounds. The weekend stay came with tickets for admission into the park. They'd packed hotdogs, and marshmallows, and all kinds of gear his father borrowed from friends who did camp. It took over an hour to set up the family-sized tent. The first night went all right. Sitting around the fire had been the best. They told ghost stories and made s'mores. When it was time for bed, they barely fit inside. It was hot and humid. The tent was like a sauna. The heat and humidity was nothing compared to the Congo. He hadn't known that then, though. The next two days, and nights, all it did was rain. Water made its way into the tent. Everything was wet. He felt dirty the entire time. No one else had any fun; by the last day his father used more cuss words than non-cuss words, and his mother gave up yelling at him about it.

Camping sucked. So why had he let himself get tricked into spending three months in the middle of nowhere?

And now that he was here, he was in charge. Circuitz expected him to handle operations. He was their project manager. It was a joke. They wanted him because he studied some rocks in college six or seven years ago? Weren't they going to be thrilled to hear he'd crashed the backhoe, and maybe lost a handful of employees his first day on the job?

He remembered telling himself, give it a try, it's something new, it will look great on a resume. All of those things sounded great at the time. Obviously. He was here. He was in a cabin in the jungle with twelve other people.

Yeah. He wasn't worried about getting fired. He expected it. What he wanted now, what his brain should stay focused on, is how to get home. He wanted out of this place because, basically, this just wasn't worth the money.

The door opened.

Powell looked up. He didn't realize anyone had left. Maybe he had drifted off? The cabin was still dark. He saw people scattered around the room sleeping, but none of them were mercenaries.

Ian Ross knelt next to Powell. He tapped him on the arm.

"What? I'm up."

"I'm sorry," Ian said.

"You didn't see my eyes open?" Powell said.

"It's dark. I said I was sorry."

"What's the problem?" The accent was thick. The man wasn't simple to understand.

"We have some water damage in the generator room."

Powell sat up. His back hurt. He rubbed his shoulder. "Damage? Like what?"

"Like, everything in there is completely ruined."

There was no way of pretending this was all a dream. It would be amazing if it were. He hoped he was asleep in the states. In his apartment. In his bed. Any second his alarm clock would go off, and he'd open his eyes, look at the time and cringe. But he wouldn't hit snooze. Not this time. He'd throw off the covers, sit up and stretch, savoring the day and the end of a horrific nightmare.

"Ruined, how?" Powell said.

"Part of the wall came down. Water and mud filled the room. We had the power sources up off the ground. Without a wall, didn't matter. Looks like there was a small fire, too. Electrical. Luckily it didn't spread," Ian said.

"How long until we have it up and running again?" He'd never had the chance to charge his phone. He wanted to get online desperately. He felt similar to when he quit smoking and his body demanded a cigarette, shaky and as if his last nerve was frayed.

"Immediately," Ian said.

Powell sighed. That was great news. Not at all what he expected. "Okay. Okay, good. That's good to hear."

"Immediately after we get all new equipment," Ian said. He laughed. "It's why when I told you everything is ruined, I meant, everything is ruined."

"So we have no power?"

"Nothing."

Powell got to his feet. Claire was awake, looking at them. Akia was still on the cot, his shoulder against the wall. He looked sound asleep. "Where are the others on your team?"

"They have the perimeter. Everything is secure," Ian said.

Secure from what? Powell wondered. The dig was in shambles. No one was going to raid their camp. There was nothing worth taking, apparently. They had to be the safest operation in the jungle at the moment. The thought didn't bring any consolation. "Marksman?"

"He's actually assessing the damage in the generator hut."

His clothing stunk. Dried sweat and mud. He wanted a shower and a change of clothing. Didn't make sense at the moment. He was going to have to go back into the pit and look over the backhoe. They needed a way to get the machinery up and out of the mud. He only had one idea and no idea if it could work.

"What should I do?" Claire said. She sat on the foot of the cot the two young girls slept on.

"Right now, I'm not positive. Keep an eye on the kids. They're going to wake up soon. I don't want them, or anyone leaving yet," Powell said, and walked out of the cabin.

Outside, nothing looked different. You could not tell there had been a storm. Birds sang, and monkeys made monkey noises. The jungle was alive and well. And loud. It was early morning and at least eighty degrees. The humidity must have been ninety percent, but less stifling than it had been inside the small cabin. He scanned the area looking for the mercenaries. Even dressed in all black, they blended perfectly with the trees and dense brush. He couldn't see them.

He swatted at large mosquitos as he walked around the cabin and toward the generator hut behind it. When Ian had said a wall came down, he figured it had been cracked, or ripped open. No. It was gone. The front wall was completely missing.

Marksman was bent over the batteries, a box of tools on the table beside him.

"Looks pretty bad?" Powell said.

Marksman stood up straight. He dropped a socket set into the tool box. It clattered. "There's not going to be a thing I can do. I'm going to send two people into town. Have them pick up two new batteries we can use. Won't be the same as this, but it will be better than nothing. We'll get them started after breakfast."

"So we can't contact anyone?"

"I have my cell phone, the others have theirs. We're not getting any service, though. Nothing. Storm must have knocked out towers. Not usually the best service this deep into the jungle anyway. But right now, we've got nothing," Marksman said.

Powell turned around and walked away from the hut.

"What are you going to do?"

"Check on the backhoe," he said. Powell thought he heard Marksman snicker. He wasn't sure why the two of them didn't get along, but it annoyed him. It had to be a power thing. He was a strong type A personality and clearly threatened by anyone else in authority.

Powell walked toward the pit contemplating heading into town with whomever Marksman sent for supplies. Only thing was if he went along, he would not return. He'd find a way back to a city, and locate an airport, and fly his ass across the ocean back home. He didn't dismiss the thought. He just knew if he tagged along, that was what would happen.

Standing at the mouth of the pit, he shook his head. The backhoe was on its side, and nearly half was buried in the ground. The mud wasn't dry, but drying. Letting out a long, loud sigh was about all he could do.

At the opposite end was Stacy Jennings. She waved hello. He returned the wave.

There was no point walking down into the pit. He couldn't do anything on his own. Once everyone was together, they would go down and try pushing it up right. Even from where he stood, that seemed impossible. What other options existed? Maybe they could use rope and elephants—did elephants live in the Congo? He had no idea. If there were elephants, he'd need someone who owned trained elephants. It wasn't like they could wrangle up some elephants out of a herd and bring them back to the pit—

Something came out of the woods. It was too far away for Powell to see clearly. Whatever it was, it was low to the ground. Jennings spun around, facing it. Powell heard shrieks.

He walked around the edge of the pit, watching her. She was kneeling by whatever it was. She had one hand to her ear. She might be talking. Maybe the mercenaries still had enough juice to remain in contact. He hoped so. Those batteries would run low eventually. By then maybe they would have at least one generator back up and running and could charge some of the equipment.

As Powell rounded the final corner, he noticed it was not an animal that had emerged out of the trees. It was one of the mercenaries. He couldn't tell which one.

"Hurry, Louis. I need your help," Jennings said. She had a man's head in her lap.

Powell stopped where he was. They were covered in blood.

"Louis, help me," she said.

Stacy Jennings didn't sound like the tough mercenary. For the first time he thought she sounded normal, like a lady. There was a tremble in her tone of voice, a vulnerability she must have masked behind muscle and brawn. It worked better than a commanding attitude. He ran toward her and only stopped again when a foot away.

"My God. What happened?" Powell said.

Jack Shelton was missing an arm. Jagged flesh and blood flared out from an empty socket at the shoulder. There was a long string of shredded muscle that came out of the wound. Blood spilled from the corner of his mouth, his eyes were closed.

"Is he okay?" Powell said.

"Hold his head," she said.

Powell got onto his knees. He took Shelton's head onto his lap. The man was breathing, barely.

Jennings stood up and removed her belt. "He's bleeding out."

She tied the belt tight around the shoulder and what stump was available. She pulled on the leather and fastened it. "This isn't going to hold well. It's going to have to do." Powell thought she might be talking out loud. Maybe it helped her think and stay focused? He had no First Aid training. Telling him anything wasn't going to help. He knew they needed to stop the bleeding. He assumed the belt was a makeshift tourniquet. Other than that, he didn't know what they should do. "Should we carry him?"

"I called Marksman. They're coming. We can't move him. Not like this," she said.

"What happened?"

She shook her head. Her eyes were watery. She kept pressure on the belt tension. "He came out of the woods and collapsed. He didn't say anything. I asked him. He couldn't respond, and then his eyes rolled back in his head and he collapsed."

Powell looked at the trees around them. This could have happened anywhere. How deep had he been sent to guard the perimeter? "Whatever did this could still be out there," he said. He knew whatever had attacked Shelton was still out there, not *could still be* out there. "I mean, what do we do? We can't just sit here."

"You want to leave, go."

Powell heard loud voices.

Charlie Erb ran at them with a military gurney. Marksman and Becky Robinson were right behind him. They had their rifles panning the area while they ran. Powell hoped they were as good as they looked. The mercenaries could finally be a silver lining.

Claire.

She was back at the cabin with the others.

He figured they were safe. An animal had attacked Shelton. Not a man. The missing arm wasn't the work of angry raiders. More than likely it was a hungry predator. It must have taken Shelton by surprise. Maybe it had stalked the merc and when it saw an opportunity, surprised him when it attacked. A lion could do that. A gorilla could too. Gorillas were as strong as five or ten men. Something like that. Powell needed water. His throat felt terribly dry.

Erb set the gurney down. "Ah, man," he said. "Hey buddy? Shelton?"

"He passed out," Jennings said.

"He's going to go into shock. Might already be. John, let's get him on the gurney," Erb said.

Marksman said, "Robinson, Jennings watch our backs. What happened?"

Powell watched the men carefully lift and place Shelton onto the gurney. The belt fell off the man's bleeding shoulder. "We need a better tourniquet," Erb said.

"We can't do it here. We can't help him here. Lift on three," Marksman said.

Jennings went first. She moved fast, but cautiously led them. She faced the forest. She looked anxious to shoot something. Anything. She was hungry for revenge. Her friend was in bad shape. Her eyes were narrow. She scanned the thick brush; a target. Any target seemed like it might do. Powell felt like something was getting shot sooner or later.

Robinson stayed on the side of the gurney. She held the belt tight, hopefully slowing if not stopping the bleeding altogether. Powell followed from the rear. He watched Jennings.

CHAPTER 10

They crashed through the closed cabin door. Those inside jumped back. Everyone was awake at this point. The kids cowered. Powell looked around the cabin, feeling frantic. Claire went and sat beside the young girls. Akia, Ruh and the other young man clustered close on Powell's cot.

"Ian's got the fire around back. Robinson, take two machetes and stick them in the coals," Marksman said. He took the belt and pulled tight. Shelton was losing too much blood.

Robinson snatched up two machetes and ran outside.

Marksman said, "What happened out there?"

"He just came out of the woods," Jennings said. "He dropped at my feet. I saw the blood. I guess my first thought was he'd been shot, or ambushed."

Marksman grunted.

Powell knew it was an animal attack, not an ambush. "We need to call for help. A helicopter rescue or something. We've got to get this man out of the jungle. He needs a hospital." There was no need stating the obvious. If they didn't get Jack Shelton professional help soon, he would die.

"Hey, buddy," Marksman said. "We're going to get this fixed up quick for you. Don't think you're going home, though. We've got too much work out here. I can't afford letting you head to the states while we sweat our asses off.

Uh-uh. No, sir. So let's get this bandaged up and get you back to work."

Shelton's eyes were open. They looked almost vacantly about the room. He seemed focused on the ceiling, but he grinned. That was a good sign. He'd heard Marksman's words and actually smiled. There was still hope.

"That's right, friend. That's right. Hang on. Hang in there, buddy." Marksman turned around. "Tell them I need those machetes. Now."

The cabin door banged open.

Ian Ross held both machetes. The long flat blades burned red. "Move," Ian shouted, pushing his way toward the cot, holding the blades high in the air. "I've got this. Let me do it. You guys, grab his legs."

It took Powell a moment. He wasn't sure what was happening. It came to him all at once. He wasn't sure he could watch, but didn't think he could look away. Robinson knelt on the floor and pressed all of her weight down on a leg, Jennings took the other. Erb had the one arm.

Marksman moved around and got behind Shelton's head. "Give me something to put in his mouth!"

Powell ran for the small counter. He held up a wooden spoon. "This?"

"Perfect," Marksman said. He grabbed it out of Powell's hand and set it lengthwise in Shelton's mouth. "Bite down on that."

Shelton didn't respond. Powell figured once the procedure started, the man wouldn't need instruction.

"Turn the girls away," Powell said to Claire. It was an order given just in time. Claire was between the girls, and they immediately hugged her tight, burying their faces against her chest. She held the foreheads with the palms of her hands, and winced in anticipation, closing her eyes as well.

Ian used the machete and quickly chopped away dangling chunks of flesh, muscle, and sinew. With a snap of his wrist, he freed the belt, dropped it, and pressed the flat of the first blade against the shoulder where the arm used to be. He overlapped the second blade, covering the entire and bare socket.

Flesh hissed.

Shelton screamed before his teeth bit into the spoon. The veins in his neck bulged, as if they were going to pop out through the skin. His face was red from straining. The blood was rushing to his head.

"Hold him!" Ian shouted.

The smell of cooked meat filled the inside of the cabin. Powell thought he might vomit. Robinson and Jennings relaxed their hold.

"He passed out," Marksman said.

"No," Ian said. "He's not breathing."

"He's breathing," Marksman said. He removed the spoon and lowered his ear next to Shelton's mouth.

"Is he breathing?" Jennings said.

"I'm listening," Marksman said.

"He's not. He's not breathing," Ian said.

"You're right. He's not. Get him on the floor," Marksman said.

Ian dropped the machetes. The flesh was blackened, red and raw. He grabbed the mercenary and dropped him onto the floor. Ian tipped Shelton's head back, placing one hand under his neck. He lowered his head down close, listening for breathing.

"The AED," Ian shouted. Jennings grabbed a small light blue case from a shelf. She knelt beside Ian. "John, cut open his shirt!"

Marksman tore open Shelton's vest, pulled a Bowie knife from the sheath on his hip and ran it down the black t-shirt.

Ian removed two rectangular patches from the case. He affixed one by the heart, the other on Shelton's side. He charged the machine. "Stand back," he said.

When the light turned green on the automated external defibrillator indicator, he pressed a red button. Shelton's body didn't move. Powell expected it to jump or arch the way it oftentimes did on medical television shows.

"Again," Ian said out loud. He waited for the red light to switch to green. Once it did, he said, "Stand back."

No one had gotten close.

Ian pressed the button. Powell knew volts raced through Shelton's body in an attempt at restarting the heart. Ian listened for breathing. He stared at Shelton's chest hoping to see it rise and fall. He tore off the patches, shoved away the AED case before pinching Shelton's nose closed, and blew two quick breaths into his mouth. Shelton's chest rose with each breath. The airway was clear. He set the heel of his left hand on Shelton's chest, between the nipples, and the other hand on top of the first. Up on his knees, Ian started compressions. He counted them off fast. "One, two, three, four, five..."

Jennings stood over Ian Ross. She chewed on the skin around her thumb, ignoring the tears that ran down her face.

Ian stopped.

Marksman leaned in, and while holding Shelton's nose closed, blew two more breaths into his mouths. The lungs filled. The chest rose.

Ian started counting off compressions again. Sweat covered his brow. He pressed fast and hard. Bone snapped. Ribs were cracking inside Shelton's chest.

Becky Robinson sat by Shelton's boots. She stared at them performing CPR. She looked ready to jump in.

Powell was frozen by the counter where he'd grabbed the spoon for Shelton to bite down on. Everything since last night had become surreal. How could all of this be happening? "The phone? Someone needs to call for help. We need to be lifted out of here!"

Claire stood up. She kept the young girls close and led them out of the cabin. The young men followed behind them.

Powell still couldn't move. He had never seen CPR performed. He had never seen a man lose an arm.

He had never seen a man die.

Ian breathed heavily.

Robinson moved around Shelton's legs. When Ian stopped, and Marksman blew two more breaths into Shelton's lungs, Robinson took over with compressions. Jennings handed Ian a bottle of water.

"Should we get a phone?"

"They're broken, Louis. Everything was ruined in the rain," Ian said. "They were in the generator hut. They don't work."

Powell almost laughed. It sounded like a joke. It was rain. Sure it had stormed, but weren't satellite phones durable? Hell, his cell phone could take a pretty good licking and still worked. How was it possible that everything was falling apart so completely, so fast?

"He's gone," Marksman said.

"We're not giving up," Robinson said. She gave hard, quick thrusts.

How many ribs were broken?

Marksman sat back. "He's gone. He's dead."

"He's not dead, John! I'm not stopping. Get ready to blow into his mouth," she said. She wasn't counting out loud. Maybe she was keeping track inside her head. "Ready, and now."

She stopped the compressions. Marksman didn't move. His hands were on Shelton's temples.

"Blow into his mouth!" Robinson shot her boss a look of insane anger. Her eyes were narrowed and brow furrowed. She looked like she was ready to fight. "Fine. Fuck you!"

Becky Robinson leaned forward and shoved Marksman backward. Powell didn't expect him to fall away. He did, though. Robinson tilted Shelton's head, pinched closed his nose and then blew two deep breaths into Shelton's mouth.

"Becky," Jennings said.

Robinson ignored Stacy Jennings. She positioned herself over Shelton's chest and resumed compressions.

Marksman stood up, slowly. He looked at Jennings, his lips pursed, and frowning.

Powell didn't think he could watch much more. The man was dead. They all knew it. He had lost too much blood, and cauterizing the wound was more than the man could take. Clearly in shock, Shelton's body gave up.

Marksman walked behind Robinson.

CPR had been in progress for nearly half an hour at this point. There was no bringing the man back.

# # #

Louis Powell walked outside with his head hung low, all of his senses on overload. The ground was saturated. His boots made a sucking sound in the mud with every step he took. He could still smell Shelton's cooked flesh. He wasn't sure he'd ever not be able to smell it. The animals in the jungle whooped and cawed, chirped and howled around him, but it came across muffled as if he cupped his hands over his ears, distorting all sound. His vision was blurred.

Sweat mixed with tears and seemed to sit stagnate around his eyeballs.

"Louis?" Claire said.

Powell looked up. The sky was grey. It didn't look like rain, though. It just looked like completely grey skies. The jungle was green. Full of thriving life. The storm strengthened its plushness. He couldn't fathom the creatures and insects that thrived in this place. He knew there were undiscovered species everywhere, if only he knew what to look for. Maybe anthropology, or anything other than geology, would have been a better course of study.

"Louis," she said again, stepping toward him.

He couldn't talk. He knew if he tried speaking, he'd break down. He didn't want to lose it. Keeping it together was going to be essential. Like it or not, they had some decisions to make. Or he did, anyway. If, that is, he truly was in charge of the operation.

Powell shook his head.

He saw the small glimmer of hope like a sparkle go flat in Claire's eyes.

She wrapped arms around him and lowered her head onto his chest. Her cold tears soaked through his thin shirt. He felt them wet his skin.

He hugged her back, looking past her at the young girls. What was he going to do with them?

CHAPTER 11

There was a slight breeze. Nothing moved in it. The trees stood tall, and green, and still. It did nothing to chase away the thick humidity, either. Louis Powell looked around at the pit, and the cabin, and at everyone gathered outside. He knew they expected leadership. Marksman was more than capable and definitely more experienced. Leaving decisions up to the mercenary might prove easiest, Powell just wasn't sure he'd agree with those decisions. The only way to ensure things went according to plan—his plan—was if he was the one calling the shots.

"We're going to do two things." Powell closed his mouth and made eye contact with Claire. He wasn't sure if he'd actually spoken out loud. She stared at him, as if waiting for him to continue, verifying he had indeed said what he'd been thinking. "We need to get these kids home, and then we're going to get a ride back into town."

"Town?" Claire said.

"We're leaving. Headed back to the states. This stint of the company dig is over." He was about to become unemployed. It didn't matter. When he started job hunting, and was asked why he was no longer employed with Circuitz, he was confident his explanation for termination would be one hundred percent absolved. "Once they have things...under control inside, I want you to pack up our bags, Claire. I'll talk with Marksman. We're leaving as soon as possible, while it's early enough in the morning and we can get the most of traveling by foot."

He didn't want to go back into the cabin. The mercenaries were gathered and mourning the loss of their friend. They deserved time alone. Thing was, he cared, but not enough to risk losing anymore daylight. Knocking lightly, he entered.

"Marksman," Powell said. "We need to talk."

They had covered Jack Shelton's body with a blanket. The floor was still covered in blood. The defibrillator case was open, the adhesive pads and wires strewn about. Stacy Jennings was seated on a cot in a corner, knees drawn up, arms wrapped around them; Becky Robinson stood by the window, back to the wall, staring vacantly at the covered corpse. The most disturbing was Charlie Erb, who knelt at Shelton's feet, his hands on Shelton's covered legs, as if praying. Nothing wrong with praying. Powell just didn't think that was what the man was doing.

"Outside," Marksman said.

They walked out and around to the back of the cabin.

"We need to get the workers back home to their families," Powell said.

"Not our job," Marksman said. "What else?"

Powell cocked his head to the side. "Not our job?"

"Getting them home is not our job. Do you have something else you want to discuss, because right now my friends and I are trying to figure out arrangements for Jack."

Arrangements? Powell thought. "We're leaving. We need you to get Claire and I back to an airport."

Marksman laughed.

"Is something funny?" Powell said.

"Yes. You. You want to go home, is that it? Feeling a little homesick?"

Powell didn't like Marksman's tone of voice. "This has been a disaster since we arrived. We're not going to be able to dig. We've got a machine sinking in the mud. The coltan is going to have to wait."

"Brunson is not going to be happy about that," Marksman said. "But I don't give a fuck about him right now. Or the company. Shelton is dead. He's dead. We're going to have to carry him to town. You and Ms. Askew are more than welcome to tag along, and if you want to get to an airport after that, fine. But I am not worrying myself, or my men, with the task of getting those people back home."

"Kids. They're just children, Marksman. They have families who are probably worried sick about them. We're going to get them back home," Powell said.

Marksman stepped in close. "Are you telling me what I'm going to do?"

He wasn't sure where the courage came from. The blood inside his body was pumping hard and fast, surging through his body. "That's exactly what I'm doing. I'm the project manager—"

"What the fuck is that supposed to mean?"

Powell didn't want to completely alienate Marksman. Their training and knowledge of the jungle was the only guarantee he had they would escape unharmed. They had the weapons, and the skills to protect them. The last thing he wanted to risk was thrusting a barrier between them. If his life hung in the balance, he needed reassurance Marksman and the other mercs would help.

"We just want to get out of here. We'll come with you into town. Maybe that will be enough. I'm just concerned about the kids," Powell said.

Marksman's look softened. His eyes weren't as narrowed. His shoulders loosened up some and relaxed. "We'll get you to town," Marksman said. He looked up at the sky, around at the trees. "I've about had it with this place, with this assignment. I think we're ready for a new employer. I don't have an issue with the Congo. I am just tired of babysitting whiny little shits who took off their dress shirt and tie and think they can come into my land and tell me what to do."

The shot was direct, Powell thought, but irrelevant. All that mattered was the mercenaries were bringing Jack Shelton's body back to town, and that he and the others could follow along. He didn't want Marksman as an enemy, but at this point, he didn't really care. "Great. We'll get our stuff together," Powell said, and walked away.

# # #

Charlie and Becky secured Jack Shelton's body onto the gurney with hooked bungee rope. The mercs wore backpacks filled with weapons. Powell watched them stuff grenades, handguns, boxes of ammo, and knives into the pouches. They kept assault rifles over their shoulders, handguns in holsters, and hunting knives strapped to their side, and thighs. Marksman, Stacy and Ian also had machetes.

Powell felt extremely inadequate. He had a knife, gloves, his boots, and a backpack of clothing and medicine, but little else. "Can you translate to the employees for me, John? I would appreciate it. Tell them we are headed to town, and they can follow us, and they can take off as we come close to their homes or villages."

Marksman said a few words, and started walking.

"Hey," Powell said. "Did you tell them what I said?"

"Did you just watch me do it?" Marksman said.

"It just seemed a little...short."

"You speak French?" Marksman said.

"No."

"Then shut the fuck up and let's go. We have a day and a half of walking ahead of us. That's when we're all walking on our own. Carrying Jack is going to slow us down. We're going to be lucky if we only have to spend two nights in the jungle before we make it back to the Jeeps."

Powell did not want to spend one night in the jungle. He hadn't felt safe inside the rickety cabin. Something bit off Jack Shelton's arm. The hairs on the back of his neck and along his arm stood on end. He couldn't shake the feeling they were being watched. He held his machete in his right hand. It was a long, eighteen-inch blade, a rubber handle. For what it was worth, he considered it a sword. He'd swing it at anything that came at him as if his life depended on it.

Seeing Charlie and Becky walk by with Jack Shelton on the gurney, he knew his life just might depend on it.

CHAPTER 12

Powell and Claire tried keeping the young workers close as they made their way along the worn path through the jungle. Powell knew the natives were accustomed to walking through the trees. This was home to them. And while they might be unnerved by Shelton's death, they probably didn't fear the...environment. At least not in the same way Powell did. His muscles twitched anxiously, as if ready for anything. That couldn't be further from the truth. He wasn't prepared for a single thing. Panicking, that was about all. He knew his breathing was quick and shallow. The animals whooped and hollered around them. He felt like they might all be talking, planning an attack.

All Powell could think about was Akia freaking out over having seen something in the trees.

Akia and Ruh walked side by side, they mumbled back and forth. Clearly, they were spooked, their environment or not. The third man walked just behind the two young girls. The three of them were silent, watching their feet, stepping carefully over congested brush. Powell, Claire, and the mercs not carrying Shelton on a gurney, worked their machetes hacking at low-hanging branches and swinging at large leaves in the way.

Powell hated how much he was sweating. The salty drops rolled down his forehead and into his eyes. He ignored the irritating sting it caused.

Marksman had point. He led the group from the Circuitz camp through the woods. When he stopped walking, he did not make a sound, but gestured for Charlie and Becky to set Shelton's body down. He made some hand signals. Fists and pointing.

Powell was lost. The other mercs knew his form of sign language. While he wanted to ask what was going on, he knew if Marksman was keeping silent, then he shouldn't speak. Obviously, Marksman sensed trouble. That was the bottom line. Protectively, he stepped closer to Claire. He scanned the tree lines around them. It was so dense. For the most part, he couldn't see past the first cluster of leaves. Fat mosquitoes buzzed around his head, attracted to his sweat-slicked skin.

Powell's heart beat fast. He didn't sense a single thing out of the ordinary. He couldn't see a single thing that didn't belong. He trusted Marksman's intuition. Standing as still as possible, he wondered what danger lurked off the path.

And then he heard it. A branch snapped. It came from the right side. Everyone looked in that general direction, guns raised. Powell wasn't sure what was out there, but it caught Marksman's attention. For that reason alone, Powell became unnerved.

No one said a word. The silence lingered. Powell strained to hear anything, everything.

Marksman gave more hand commands. Fingers up. Down. Closed first. Pointed ahead of them and behind.

Shelton's gurney was set down on the ground.

The mercenaries looked eager, as if they had been deprived of action for too long. There was a hunger in their eyes. Powell couldn't understand it. He was sure if they looked at him, the only thing they'd see was fear.

Charlie and Becky walked on ahead. Ian and Stacy went back the way they'd just come. All four were swallowed by branches with bright green leaves.

Powell couldn't hear the monkeys. The rain forest animals all fell silent. It couldn't be a good sign. It was as if the entire jungle and Marksman were in tune with each other, and all of them were aware of an unwanted predator. He took a step closer to Claire and the young girls.

The man with them patted himself on the chest and whispered, "Kacancu."

Powell bit down on his upper lip and nodded. "Shhh."

Kacancu nodded and pursed his lips tight.

Marksman waved them all in close. They gathered in a circle around him. He knelt down.

"What's going on?" Powell watched Claire taking care of the girls. She kept an arm around each of them. They clung to her as if she were their mother, at the very least, an aunt.

"We're being followed. I noticed it almost from the moment we left the cabin." Marksman then spoke French. The workers nodded. Akia rolled his fingers into his palms. His eyes were opened wide. He looked over everyone, and into the trees. "The two teams are scoping out the area. Could just be an animal."

Powell waited for the French translation before he said, "But that's not what you think?"

Marksman shook his head. "We've caught some chatter from other dig locations. Security is sending out warnings. There is a lot of theft going on. The price of raw coltan is through the ceiling. Panning the riverbeds just doesn't produce enough. The foreign companies leasing chunks of land have the deep pockets for that kind of investment. The raiders let the people excavate the land, do all of the dirty work and heavy lifting, and then they swoop in and steal the coltan. They're not afraid of confrontation, either. They'll shoot first and not bother asking questions later."

"But we left the dig. We don't have coltan with us," Claire said. "Why follow us? What could they hope to get from us?"

Rustling along the path made them all stop talking, turn and stare.

Stacy and Ian stepped forward, parting branches with the backs of arms. They fell in on the group, each taking a knee. "No sign of anything back that way," Ian said.

"We doubled back, ventured into the thicket for a bit. Nothing," Stacy said.

Marksman opened his mouth to say something. Gunfire erupted from ahead of them. He stood up and gripped his assault rifle in both hands.

Ian and Stacy jumped to their feet. They took up position on the east and west.

Powell and the others remained huddled together. The girls began crying. He knew that Kacancu introduced himself because doing so had taken his mind off being afraid, if only for the moment. This time Powell touched his chest and said to the young girls, "Louis. Louis."

The smallest girl wiped tears from her eyes. She placed her palm on Powell's chest. "Louis."

Powell smiled, and nodded encouragingly. "Yes. That's right."

Gently, Powell removed the girls hand and set it on her own chest.

The girl said, "Mangeni."

Powell's smile widened. "Mangeni."

Mangeni offered up a wide grin. "Louis."

Powell repeated his name for the other girl. She understood what they were doing. She first looked around, as if not comfortable talking when only moments ago the silence was shattered by the sound of multiple gunshots. "Nafula."

"Nafula," Powell said. "And this is Claire. Claire."

"I've introduced myself already."

"Shh!" Marksman had a finger up to his lips. His eyes were narrowed. He looked pissed that they were all talking.

He was right to be pissed. Powell had just been trying to find a way to comfort the girls. They were so small. He was sure if he had to he could pick one up in each arm. Mangeni couldn't weigh more than seventy pounds, Nafula eighty, maybe. He had no intention of picking either one up.

Something came at them. The sound of branches snapping grew louder. Whatever it was, it was moving fast. The problem was isolating the sound. Sound echoed and bounced all over the place.

Ian got to a knee. He aimed his rifle, ready to shoot at what ever got close. Stacy motioned for the rest of them to back up.

Powell couldn't help but look down at Shelton's covered body. It didn't seem right leaving a dead man on the ground. There was nothing else they could do at the moment.

Marksman remained standing. He panned left and right, and left. His finger was inside the guard on the trigger, ready to unload lead into whatever crashed through the trees.

Powell did feel safer having the mercenaries with them.

"It's us! It's us!"

It sounded like Becky. Her voice was high-pitched and frantic sounding. Powell didn't know the woman well enough. From just those two words repeated twice, he knew something was wrong. Something was very wrong.

The three mercs did not lower their weapons. It didn't matter who was calling out to them, or what they were saying. Powell saw that Marksman looked more tense than he had when he wasn't sure what approached.

It was over fast.

Becky and Charlie plowed through the trees. They weren't on the path. They came at the gathered group, jumping over downed trees.

Charlie Erb yelled, "Get back to the cabin. Go! Go!"

No one moved. Powell wanted to. He had no idea why these two mercenaries wanted everyone to return to the cabin, but if they thought doing so was safer than being out in the open, he was all for it.

Marksman held up a halting hand. "We wait," he said.

Charlie reached them first. He bent over, hands on his knees. He breathed fast and hard.

Becky said, "There's a fucking dinosaur out there."

Powell thought of the K-Rex. He couldn't imagine a giant prehistoric beast trampling through the trees. He'd seen enough movies about dinosaurs. Even the Godzilla films, along with all of the remakes. It was preposterous. Those things just didn't exist anymore, and Godzilla never existed. He almost laughed at the explanation.

Claire said, "There's no such th—"

Powell saw something then. "You know about it," he said, looking at Marksman. "Whatever is out there, you already know about it."

Becky shook her head. "He couldn't know about this. I'm no expert on fucking dinosaurs, but the thing was about seven feet tall, and long. The tail was real long, like from head to tail, the thing had to be eighteen, nineteen feet." She had her arms stretched out wide illustrating the size of the thing, her rifle dangled by the strap over her shoulder, the muzzle pointed at the ground. "Fucker had short arms with talons, and ran on its two hind legs. Know what I think, I mean, do you want to know what I think it was? We saw a velociraptor. A fucking velociraptor is running wild in the Congo! We're not going anywhere but back."

"Grab Shelton," Marksman said.

Powell was furious. Marksman was ignoring him. The man knew about *whatever* it was out in the forest. It sure as shit wasn't any dinosaur.

"We need to get these kids back to their families," Claire said.

Marksman pointed forward. "I know they live that way. You want to take them back, be my guest. We're headed back to the cabin. I suggest you do the same."

Going back didn't make sense. "What aren't you telling us?" Powell said.

"Look," Charlie Erb said. "I saw the thing, too. Robinson's not lying. She's not exaggerating."

"I'm not doubting her," Marksman said. "We're closer to the cabin than we are to any village. Safest thing to do right now is get back to the cabin and figure a way to fix the radios."

"Why?" Powell said.

"Why, what?" Marksman said.

"There's dinosaurs out there. For real. Jurassic Fucking Park beasts in this jungle," Powell said.

"Yes, there are," Marksman said.

Powell wasn't expecting that. He thought for sure the merc would deny the crazy allegation. "We should keep moving. We should get these kids home, and we should get out of the jungle, John. Going back is a bad idea."

"There's more than one," Marksman said. "These things don't hunt alone. They hunt in packs. I've never seen more than three together at any given time. It's been known to happen. They are not dumb creatures with peanut-sized brains. The velociraptor is a cunning, calculating, and conniving son of a bitch. No one knew that when they first started gluing together dug up bones, but I've seen them. I've watched them hunt. For all we know right now, we're surrounded." He held out his arms and spun around in a circle. "I know they're out there watching us. They have been following us since we left the cabin."

"You knew it wasn't raiders."

"There are no raiders. No one is getting robbed. It's easier telling the public, and the employers, that groups of armed bandits steal the coltan, and shoot up the miners. Can you imagine the pandemonium if we told the world velociraptors were loose and eating people?"

"You never told us," Becky said. "Not once did you mention this to us. To any of us."

Ian looked down at his boots. "I knew."

"This is not the time," Marksman said. "Grab Shelton. We need to move slow, but steady. No sudden movements. No running. No noise."

The only thing Powell wanted to do more than leave the Congo was run screaming back to the cabin. He was torn. He was still convinced going forward was better. "You have the guns. The bullets," Powell said. "We need to get out of here. We need to get the kids back home to their families."

"You said that already, Mr. Powell."

"But you're ignoring me."

"I'm done talking. Grab Shelton, or don't. I'm going back," Marksman said, and he started walking back toward the cabin.

Becky continued staring at Ian, slowly shaking her head. She looked disgusted. Powell understood. Keeping a secret from your team was horrible. It was worse when you considered each other friends. She must have felt betrayed, Powell thought.

"What do we do?" Claire said.

Powell looked down the path in both directions. If he knew the lay of the jungle, and was any kind of an outdoorsman, he'd lead them out of the trees and back to some kind of civilization. However, he wasn't. Only way he knew to start a fire was by using a lighter. He had no idea what was okay to eat, or what was poisonous. "We go back to the cabin."

"Come on, kids," Claire said, herding the five older children.

No one took the time explaining what was going on to the workers. Marksman seemed like the only one who spoke their language. They needed to know what was going on. He knew they had to be even more frightened for that reason. He was surprised though, when not one of them protested, and simply followed Claire's lead.

The mercs were behind Powell. They kept their weapons trained on the trees.

"You fired at one of them?" Ian asked Charlie.

"Becky did. I think she hit it, too. It went down. It wasn't dead. She hadn't killed it, but it went down and we ran. I mean, we saw that thing, and it saw us. I hesitated. I couldn't get my mind around what I was seeing. Not Becky. Fuck. She just let loose some rounds and, ka-blam, its blood went spraying and it dropped," Charlie said, as they walked behind Powell.

He didn't mean to eavesdrop, but it seemed like the only way to gather some honest information. However, hearing Charlie Erb's rendition didn't help any, because if he was telling the truth, and Becky was telling the truth, then velociraptors were stalking them.

Powell knew when he agreed to take the project manager assignment that things could get hairy in the jungle. He wasn't stupid. The fact he was being sent to the Congo made him apprehensive from the get-go. He knew the humidity, and rain, and animals, and insects would all be a problem. All of it. His brain accepted those variables. But velociraptors? Did that even make sense?

Velociraptors, and somehow John Marksman already knew.

Ian knew, too.

Who else knew?

Did Circuitz know?

Of course they did. Marksman would have reported it. The mercenary probably negotiated more money out of the deal. Maybe they asked him for some proof and he provided it, and they gave him more money.

"What are you thinking?" Claire said.

"My mind's just...it's whirling around like a tornado inside my skull. I have no idea what is in the forest. I'm just not ready to accept sight unseen that dinosaurs are here. I can't," Powell said.

Akia tapped Powell on the shoulder and pointed at Shelton. He stretched his arms out on front of him and made them scissor up and down, his fingers on both hands meshing together like gnashing teeth, as if imitating a crocodile bite, and then he roared.

Marksman, Ian, and Akia knew about the dinosaur.

It was near impossible walking slowly. Louis Powell's legs wanted to run. He felt it each time his foot left the ground. His insides were coiled and ready to spring. A few things kept him from dashing ahead. One, he didn't think the cabin would provide much safety. It was a structure they could hole up in. The mercs were heavily armed and could defend the makeshift fortress, but without any form of communication with the outside world, what difference did it make? How long would it be before anyone came looking for them? Two, he wouldn't leave Claire and the kids. While the mercs could, and would do a better job protecting them, he felt a level of responsibility. He might be a coward, and scared shitless in this God forsaken jungle, but he wasn't an asshole. Their lives mattered to him. He would do everything he could to keep everyone safe, even if that only filtered out to little less than taking command of the operation. The third, and perhaps biggest reason of all for why he didn't run back toward the cabin, was because of the predators stalking them. He was not ready to believe dinosaurs still existed, or that velociraptors lived in the dense rainforest of the Congo. It was ludicrous. Was something big, and powerful, and dangerous out there beyond the path? More than likely, yes. The mercs were unnerved. That spoke volumes. And if they were squirmy, he'd be foolish not to be.

One step at a time was how they made their way along the path. Everything was different now. When they left the cabin, Powell felt a sense of relief. They were going to get out of the Congo. He'd never return. Couple of days out here, and all he wanted was home. They had been headed toward that goal. Now? They weren't going. There was no other way to feel about that but deflated.

The sky grumbled, thunder rolling. Powell didn't even look up. The canopy was thick. It didn't matter. He did not want to even risk seeing storm clouds. He was rained out. His body and clothing hadn't felt dry since they reached this half of the world. They didn't need more rain. He wasn't sure he could handle any more. It relentlessly ate away at his sanity. There wasn't much more he could take.

Was anything following them? Were they still being watched? He had so many more questions, too many more. He knew asking Marksman now would be futile. They'd already spent far too much time talking. He wanted a gun. Someone would have to show him how to shoot, but he wanted one. The machete might be an ideal weapon for hacking at vines and branches. He couldn't see himself using it like a sword in a duel against a sharp taloned dinosaur.

He laughed.

Claire looked at him, questioningly. "What's funny?" Her voice was barely audible. The whisper fell from her lips. It was calming to Powell's ears.

"Tell you later," he said.

"Promise? Because I could use something to laugh at," she said. She smiled.

How did she manage to find the courage to smile? Everything about the situation was depressing, dark, and foreboding. Was he the only one that worried they'd all die in the forest? It didn't seem likely, but that didn't mean he wasn't worried about it. Because he was. "Promise," he said.

The cabin was right where they left it, although it looked smaller now. Powell tried to imagine the twelve of them packed in tight for the next day or two. Did they have enough food? Was there enough water?

They walked around the edge of the dig site. Powell just stared at the piece of machinery on its side. He never even attempted righting it. He never managed the dig for even a day. Not one day. He had failed at the assignment in record time. From the time he turned fourteen, he'd held a job. A paper route along the tract he'd grown up on earned him money enough to see movies, buy name brand clothing, and even save a little. Except when he was in college, he'd always been employed. And even then, he completed work study programs in order to knock cost off his tuition. He found himself looking forward to collecting unemployment when he got back to the states. Maybe he'd forfeit his lease and move back in with his parents. He'd love home-cooked meals and having his laundry done for him. He'd spend the year in bed watching Netflix or something; maybe catch up on bestselling books he'd been meaning to read for the last seven years. It sounded like the perfect plan.

"Everyone inside," Marksman said. "Keep it slow. Single file."

Powell lined the kids up behind Claire while they kept walking, and he stood behind all of them. Until he received some lessons on firing a gun properly, he held the machete like a pirate. He knew he was grinding his teeth. His jaw felt sore. His mouth was dry. His eyes panned left and right. He was doing his best to be ready. The last thing he wanted was to be caught by surprise. At any moment he expected...well, a fucking dinosaur...to charge them.

It didn't happen. They all made it into the cabin.

He had let his imagination get the better of him. His mind had conjured veil images of mass carnage. His heart had never beat so fast or so hard inside his chest before. He was moving on pure adrenaline at this point. It was what kept him going. It might be the only thing that truly allowed him to be led back to the cabin.

He couldn't get over it, or let it go. This had been the wrong move. Coming back to the cabin was a mistake. He only hoped he was wrong and that Marksman was right. Because if anything happened to any of the kids, or to Claire...

CHAPTER 13

Powell hoped the angry sky would just pass. He was wrong. It was there to stay.

It was maybe a half hour after they reached the cabin that the daylight was completely chased from above, and heavy black clouds blanketed the Congo. Behind the clouds, static electricity bounced back and forth. No bolts had yet been released. And for the moment, the rain did not fall. It was just a matter of time, he supposed.

The mercs stood guard by the windows.

No one talked much.

The workers whispered back and forth. Powell wished he understood their conversations. He felt helpless. Their families had to be worried.

Powell ran his palms down his thighs and stood up straight. He let out a long, loud sigh. "So what are we doing? I mean, what are we going to do here?"

No one answered. Powell expected Marksman to reply. Nothing but silence filled the cabin.

"I want to know what's in the forest, John," Powell said. He would not be ignored. "John! I'm talking to you."

Marksman sucked in a deep breath. "We learned about the velociraptors a while back."

Powell rolled his eyes.

"Do you want an answer?" Marksman said.

"I want the truth," Powell said.

"This is the truth. It's the truth. There are velociraptors in the Congo. Always have been. The species either never died out, or somehow were given a second chance."

"A second chance?" Claire said. She stood over Mangeni and Nafula. They sat around her legs. She'd become like their mother. "From who?"

"Mother nature?" Marksman said.

"It's bullshit." Powell couldn't wrap his mind around what he heard. Something like that wouldn't be kept a secret. If living dinosaurs had been discovered, the world would know. Videos would be on YouTube, photos on Facebook. Celebrities would be tweeting about the need to save and preserve the prehistoric beasts.

"Doesn't matter where the second chance came from." Marksman sounded angry now. His face reddened. "Point is they're out there. I've been up in the mountains and watched them from a safe distance."

"And Circuitz knows about this? Brunson and legal?" Powell said.

Marksman nodded. "They know. It doesn't stop them from digging. It's why we're here. We're to protect the operation. Keep all of you safe."

"How could you not tell us?" Charlie said. "Shelton's dead. One of those things could be responsible. If he'd known about raptors in the forest, he might have carried himself differently."

"He's a professional, Erb. Same as you. Same as me. The enemy could be anywhere, could be anyone, could be anything. You are either ready, or you're not," Marksman said.

Erb got to his feet. His muscles were tight, tensed. His hands were knuckled fists. He looked like he might pop.

"Still should have shared the information with us," Stacy said. "We had a right to know."

"The less people that know the truth the better," Marksman said. "Best I can tell there aren't that many. Largest herd I've ever come across was maybe six or seven. I've seen some smaller groupings with three or four. I've never tried keeping track of them though. I could be seeing the same fucking things over and over, or maybe I've never seen the same one more than once. In this region of the Congo, it's impossible to say how many there are. I haven't got a clue what their breeding habits are, how old they live to be, or anything. They remind me of bees for the most part. You don't bother them and they won't eat you."

"Jesus," Becky said. "Do you hear yourself? You're trying to make it sound like this is all just a big nothing. Six or seven dinosaurs in a herd is six or seven more than anywhere else in the world. How could you not tell us? We have no secrets. That's how we've always operated. As a family. Erb's right. Shelton's dead, John. Dead. That's on you." She stormed out of the cabin, slamming the door behind her.

Again, no one spoke. An eerie silence filled the spaces between them.

At this point, Powell had no choice but to at least accept everything. He wasn't completely convinced, but he had to accept what he heard. He did not want to end up like Shelton. "I'm asking again, John, what are we going to do next? If those things are really out there, when's a good time to make a run for it? When?"

"They've never come this close to camp. I've never seen them by the dig."

"How do you know they're here now?" Claire said.

"I thought I saw one when we were headed out. Wasn't positive. They seem to blend in with their surroundings. I felt like we were being watched."

"But you're not sure?" Powell said.

"They were following us."

"But you *didn't* see them," Powell said. "We should have kept moving. Coming back here was a bad idea. We're worse off now. We're in more danger now."

Akia pointed at the ceiling and began talking. "Nous devrions aller dans mon village. Nous sommes en sécurité. Les dinosaures ne déranger personne. Il y a un accord en place. Nous sacrifions pour eux, ils nous laissent tranquilles. Les anciens de mon village vont nous protéger. Nous tous."

Powell stared at Marksman. "What is he saying? What is he so jumpy about?"

"He's talking gibberish," Marksman said.

"Doesn't sound like it to me. It sounds important. Like he might be trying to warn us. Or help us. What's he saying?" Powell said.

"He wants us to go to his village. He says his elders have some deal with the dinosaurs. We'll be safe with his people," Marksman said, raising his eyebrows as if saying, *See? Gibberish.*

Powell ran his hands through his hair, ready to pull it out. "Thank you," he said to Akia, if only to be polite. "Thank you."

How in the world would the elders negotiate a peace treaty with velociraptors? If he wasn't so angry, and scared, and tired, and damp, he'd laugh. He'd sit down in a corner of the cabin with his knees drawn up to his chest, and laugh.

One thought stopped him from losing it, from getting hysterical. Well. It wasn't as much a thought, as it was a question. He looked at Akia and said, "Why don't the dinosaurs attack your people? Ask him, John."

"He already told us," Marksman said.

"I'm sorry," Powell said. "I still don't speak French. Mind translating for us?"

"The villages leave food, sacrifices, for the raptors. It keeps them away from the people," Marksman said.

"Like the aboriginal natives in King Kong?" Claire said. "Tying the limbs of virgins to giant stakes?"

"I have no idea how or what they do," Marksman said. "But it works. The dinos don't go near the villagers. No more than a hyena or lion might. For the most part, the people that share the Congo with the raptors are more or less...safe."

"Shit. Shit. Shit." Powell had no idea what to do. Never had anything felt more surreal. He had no problem believing he was either at home asleep, or in a hospital bed in a coma. Maybe he'd been in a horrific car accident on his way into work. Hooked up to all kinds of life support, this nightmare he was in was now his reality. It was not only possible, it was more probable than dinosaurs and native sacrifices to keep the monsters away.

Gunfire erupted outside the cabin.

Erb looked at Stacy and reached for his rifle. "Becky!" he said.

"Ian, stay here," Marksman said.

Erb, Stacy, and Marksman ran out of the cabin.

Claire locked eyes with Powell. "What do we do?"

"You heard John. I'm keeping an eye on you. Get everyone to the center of the room. Come on," Ian said, the tremor in his accent made his words that much more difficult to understand.

"You have to show us how to use the weapons," Powell said. "I want a gun."

"You ever fired one of these?" Ian held up his handgun.

Powell shook his head.

"The rifle?"

Powell said, "No."

"Hang on to the machete."

"How hard can it be?" Powell said.

Ian chewed on his lip. "It's about safety. I don't want you shooting yourself. Or hurting someone else. That would fall on me. I don't need that shit; you see what I'm saying?"

He held up the handgun. "This is how you eject the clip. See if it has bullets. It does. You're good. This is how you load it. Pop it back in like this. Safety on. Safety off. Aim, keep both eyes open. They only close one eye in the movies. You have a better chance of hitting your target with both eyes on it. Okay? You pull the trigger. Got it?"

Powell nodded. "Got it."

Ian went to a case, spun the combination locks and opened it. He handed a gun to Powell and Claire. "Nothing against the Congolese, but they ain't getting one. Give them your machetes. They know how to use those. They practically come out of the womb with one. It's like a damned extension of their arm."

"Are we going to their village?" Claire said.

"You heard the King Kong reference?" Ian said. "You want to be that virgin tied to the posts? Not me. I'd rather make for the river. We can find a boat. I am not that big on science, but I'm thinking those fuckers aren't the best swimmers."

"How far to the river?" Powell said. It was the first plan he'd heard that made any sense. He could get behind something like that. "How hard is it to find a boat?"

"We get to the river, there will be boats. Trust me. River ain't close, but it's closer than trying to make it all the way back to where we left the SUVs," Ian said.

Everyone waited, listening. It had been several moments since the other mercs left the cabin. There had not been any more gunshots fired. In fact, it was so silent outside the cabin, it was creepy.

"What do you think is going on?" Claire said. She turned the gun over in her hands. She held it as if it were delicate glass and it might break if she weren't careful. Her fingertips traced the gun's grip. "Should we check on them?"

Powell stuffed the extra clips of ammunition into his pockets. It didn't seem like enough. At least the machete didn't run out of blade.

"We stay put. They'll be back and will let us know what's happened." Ian looked toward the window at the front of the cabin. Powell thought he looked apprehensive. The merc must be worried about Becky and the others. The merc. That wasn't the right way to think about him. Ian. Ian must be worried about Becky and the others.

"You know how to get to the river from here?" Powell said.

Ian nodded. "I do."

"Have a map?"

He shook his head. "We had everything on GPS. If you head south west, you'll come across it."

Powell shook his head and shrugged.

Ian pointed. "That way."

Powell cringed when rapid gunshots were fired. They sounded close. Someone screamed. The cry was filled with terror. More gunshots. And more, still.

Ian went to the door. "You guys stay put!"

Claire dropped to her knees. The girls hugged her, burying their faces against her chest. Claire cupped the back of their heads, keeping them close, perhaps hoping that at least made them feel safe. "You can't leave us."

"John told you to stay," Powell said as well. He did not want to lose Ian. He had no idea what was happening to the others. They needed someone with them who knew the land and who spoke English. If anything happened to all the mercenaries, they were in trouble. More trouble. He didn't want to think about that. "Ian? You can't leave us."

The man looked torn. He kept his hand on the doorknob. Powell knew he wanted to run out and start shooting. He felt an obligation to protect them, as Marksman commanded. Powell sensed he'd rather be caught up in the firefight, side-by-side with his comrades on the rain forest battlefield. Ian closed his eyes and dropped his chin to his chest. He banged the butt of his handgun against his forehead. Staying inside the cabin appeared to be killing him.

"Ian," Powell said, thinking fast. He wanted the man to feel useful. The mercenary's skills could prove essential to their very survival, especially if anything happened to the others. He didn't want to think that way, but was trying to be realistic. They were out there shooting at dinosaurs. He saw what had happened to Shelton. If there was actually a pack of velociraptors out there hunting people, it could very well just be the eight of them left. "We need to have a plan. We should be ready to do something, to go somewhere. If we have to stay inside the cabin, let's figure out what we will do next. Okay? Ian?"

Ian lowered his weapon. He opened his eyes. When he let go of the doorknob and stood up straight, he looked far more composed and sane. His brow was riddled with beads of sweat. He wiped it away with his forearm. "The river," he said.

"Exactly. The river. Let's talk this through."

CHAPTER 14

Ian Ross rifled through the cabinet filled with supplies. He tossed out items left and right. He stopped when he found a spiral notebook and a pen. "I knew we had this. No idea what for, but thought I'd seen it. One of the other Circuitz people must have brought it along for their tour and left it behind," Ian said, and then with a sharpie drew a rudimentary map of the area, labeling parts. Everyone hovered around him, and behind him, watching.

"Okay. This is us. The camp, the cabin," he said. "This was the path we were taking. At this point here, it cuts to the left. It is not nearly as well-worn a trail."

"That's not saying much. I didn't even know we were on one before," Powell said, smiling. He wanted to eliminate some tension. The stress levels were high. He was on edge. He could only surmise the others were as well. "Sorry. Go ahead."

Ian cleared his throat, as if annoyed, and then pointed the tip of the sharpie at the paper. A black dot grew as the paper absorbed the ink. "If you follow this here, a day out, you'll reach the river. Twelve, maybe fourteen hours walking. The terrain is mostly level. You will come across villages. You're going to be tempted to stop, ask for help. Fight it."

"Fight it?" Claire said.

"Not every village in the Congo welcomes white people with open arms. I'm not saying you'd be in danger. If anything, they might be intrigued by your presence. They don't often see Americans in the jungle. Thing is, some are hostile. If they see you as a threat, it won't mean shit to them if they kill you and then go about their day. And don't forget the King Kong theory. I don't think it's a joke. I think it happens. A lot," Ian said.

Powell's tongue felt dry. He tried swallowing. There was no spit in his mouth.

Akia and Ruh began talking. They took turns saying something to each other. Ruh knelt down by the hand-drawn map. He pointed at the trail Ian outlined and followed it to the river. He shook his head.

"What's he saying? What's he mean?" Powell said.

"Not a fucking clue," Ian said.

Akia made a motion like he was paddling a canoe, pushing an imaginary oar through the water on one side of the craft, and then on the other.

"River? The river?" Ian said and pretended he was swimming in water.

Akia nodded. "Oui, oui."

"That means yes," Claire said.

Powell almost rolled his eyes. Everyone knew *oui* meant yes. It would have been easy to bark at her. He bit his tongue instead. She was trying to be helpful. He knew as much.

Ruh traced his finger on the paper from the cabin to the river. It was more of a straight line. Then he backed up and pointed to an unmarked spot on the map, and then to himself and the young girls. He pointed to another unmarked spot on the map, and then at Kacancu and at Akia.

"That must be where they live," Claire said.

Ian sighed. It came out sounding like a groan. "They want to go home."

"Can you blame them?" Powell said. "If their elders truly have some kind of arrangement with the raptors, out here they're in danger. We have an obligation to get them home. Safely."

"I have an obligation to save my own ass," Ian said.

Powell stood over Claire and the young girls. "Then you better do what you have to do. I'm going to get these people home, and then we'll find a way to reach that river, even if we have to do it without your help."

"Without me?" Ian said and snickered.

"I'd prefer all of us doing it together," Powell said. He hated the cocky way the merc laughed at them. All brawn and brass. While in this particular situation it made their skills appealing, he hated this kind of guy. They always managed to get under his skin, irritating him with such ease. "And I think I'm going to need your help convincing John that this might be the best course of action."

"You haven't sold me. And I'm the easy one. Convincing John, now that will be a hard sell," Ian said. "I don't think you get it. We're trying to be cool about this. We don't want to stand here and lecture just for the sake of scaring the shit out of you. Things are not good. I've seen these monsters. They're fast. They're smart. And worst of all, they're fierce. We've got limited supplies, and as of right now, we're pretty much stranded in a part of the world where by the time someone decides to come looking for us, it'll be too fucking late. These people," Ian motioned toward the natives with a wave of his hand, "they live here. They grew up here. They know what's what. You see what I'm saying? We can let them get home on their own. They'll be fine. They've been surviving inside this jungle since forever. They'll continue to do so long after we've gone. You want me to help convince John, shit son, you have no clue who we are, do you?"

Powell swallowed. His mouth was dry. His throat hurt. He didn't want to wince. What he needed was more water. It was part of the limited supplies Ian had mentioned. He knew things were bad. He wasn't stupid. However, hearing it all outlined made it more real; made it far worse. He could clam up, and not reply to Ian's rant, but that showed weakness. He did not want to lose ground. The command was his, if he was man enough to hang onto the rung. "Well, regardless. It's what we're going to do," Powell said.

Ian shook his head, smiling. Powell thought this was actually a good sign. It meant Ian thought he was a little bit crazy. The mercs respected crazy best he could tell.

"We're not going anywhere until we know what's going on out there," Ian said.

Powell almost grinned when Ian said *we're*. That was another great sign. "That's a given."

"I don't want to leave anyone behind. We need to account for everyone before we do anything. Agreed?" Ian said. His tune had changed. It was hard for Powell not to consider this a small victory. He'd savor the moment, but celebrate it later after everyone was safe and away from the threat of flesh eating dinosaurs.

Powell nodded. He wasn't sure how they could do that. The other mercenaries could be anywhere. The jungle went on and on forever, it seemed. If no one returned, did Ian expect them to first track down the others?

He didn't want to let go of hope. He prayed the others were safe, and unharmed, and out in the trees chasing shadows. The way his stomach flipped and flopped, he didn't think that was the case. He had an uneasy feeling about...well, about everything.

"First things first, I need to find out what's going on out there."

Powell realized he hadn't heard any gunshots since they started discussing the routes on the hand drawn map. That could be a good sign. More than likely it was not. He wondered what went through Ian's mind. The merc stood by the door, listening.

Claire and the others remained huddled close together.

Ian said, "Wait here. I'll be right back."

Powell didn't like that. They had done enough waiting. They were losing daylight. He was not looking forward to a thirteen hour walk through the rain forest. The last thing he wanted was completing the trek in the dark. He held up his handgun. "We're coming with you."

Powell ushered everyone out of the cabin behind Ian Ross. Claire held her handgun in both hands. They trembled. He worried she might accidentally squeeze the trigger until he noticed, thankfully, her fingers were outside of the trigger guard. So instead he worried she might drop the weapon. If it wasn't one thing, it was another. His mind was full of worry. He couldn't recall a single time in his life he'd ever been this scared. Thinking about other things—like Claire dropping her gun—was actually something of a welcome distraction. He needed an image, any image, to chase away the memories of Shelton's mangled corpse, and the lingering pungent odor of his seared flesh in a failed attempt to cauterize the massive wound and stop the bleeding.

He concentrated on his breathing. He didn't want to hyperventilate. When he was a kid, it happened a lot. His mother made him breathe in and out into a paper bag. That never helped. He'd tried telling her as much. She didn't want to hear it. The technique was all over the internet at some point. When she read something on the internet, it became gospel. Eventually, he learned ways to calm himself down. The easiest way was by simply by focusing on his breathing. Mentally slowing his heartbeat down. In and out. In and out. It worked, and that was what mattered.

He tried it now. Breathing. Concentrating on his heartbeat.

"Keep everyone close," Powell said. He looked around the dig site. Everything became surreal. It reminded him of a giant movie screen. IMAX. It wasn't too difficult to accept he was actually in a plush leather seat inside a theatre. If he tried hard enough, he might believe he could smell popcorn. Buttered.

He was losing it. His mind was slipping away. He wanted to laugh. He needed to laugh. The somber and desperate nature surrounding them was like the humidity. It was all encompassing. He was being swallowed by it. Devoured.

Ian moved ahead of them, keeping low to the ground. He held his rifle in both hands. The shoulder strap was wrapped around a forearm. He stepped heel to toe for each foot. He was quiet, although everything was wet, muddy. There wasn't much that would crunch under foot. The natives followed suit. They stayed low and moved swiftly.

Where were the others?

Powell was almost afraid of the answer. He didn't want to stumble on more remains. He didn't think his brain could process it. There was only so much more he could take. He wondered how soldiers handled war. He couldn't imagine being eighteen and shipped off to fight enemies on foreign soil. It was why he didn't join the military after high school. He knew war wasn't something he'd been built for, and yet here he was.

Looking over his shoulder, Powell kept expecting to see someone or something sneaking up on him. As much as he hated to admit it, he could only envision a stupid dinosaur behind him. It made it very difficult controlling his breathing. He knew it was a panic attack coming on. Fight or flight mentality. Everything inside of him screamed, "Run!"

There was nowhere to run.

Who was he kidding? There was nowhere to run. There was no chance they'd get away.

"Where are the others?" Powell said.

Claire looked back at him. Her eyes were open too wide, looked too wild.

She was losing it, too.

Did he look to her the way she looked to him? "Where are the other mercenaries?"

He knew Claire didn't have an answer to his question. He knew it, but he asked anyway.

Ahead of them, Ian stopped. He motioned for everyone to get lower. He was practically on his belly in the mud. He waved for Powell to come up to the front of the line.

"Keep eyes behind us. I don't want anything sneaking up on us," Powell said to Claire. "Okay?"

She nodded.

He passed the native employees, crawled up on his belly and stopped beside Ian. "What? You see something?"

"I don't see shit. I don't hear shit. I am not sure where the others are."

"So what do we do?" Powell said.

"Get that kid who was pointing all over my map and have him start you guys toward the river," Ian said.

"And what about you?"

"I'm not leaving my friends, Louis. I can look for them better on my own. I don't need an entourage. You guys will just slow me down or give away my location making noise," Ian said.

None of them had made a sound. He was pointlessly throwing stones. Whatever. "So you're leaving us?"

"Man the fuck up, Powell, will ya? You're all about getting them all home, so do it. Get them all home. We'll rendezvous at the river. Same spot I highlighted on the map. Got it?"

"I don't think this is a good idea. Splitting up can't be the right thing to do. I mean, you know that right? You know that splitting up is a horrible plan," Powell said. He felt his mind unravel. Frayed ends came loose.

Ian shook his head as he gripped Powell's shirt into a balled fist. "We don't have time to dick around, Powell. We're losing sunlight. My friends are out there. Who knows what kind of trouble they're in. They might need me. They could be in some serious shit right now. Their very lives might depend on me showing up and blowing the fuck out of shit, okay? And you know what's stopping me from doing that, from saving them? You are, asshole. You. So go on now, get the fuck out of here. Get them back to their villages if you want, and meet me at the river."

Powell stared into eyes that were as dark as the coltan they mined. He knew he'd never change the merc's mind. He just wasn't sure he could lead. Giving direction to the mercs, calling the shots, that was one thing. Leading was quite another.

A single gunshot rang out from somewhere deep inside the forest. The sound echoed. It was near impossible to pinpoint where the sound came from.

"Go on. Get out of here. I mean it, go. I've got this," Ian said. "And Powell, keep your eyes open. You at the front. Claire at the back end. Those fuckers are cunning as shit."

CHAPTER 15

Louis Powell ran toward Claire, looking over his shoulder and catching a glimpse of Ian Ross just as he was swallowed up by leaves and branches. The man *was* brave. Only certain people could run at danger when everyone else moved away from it. Powell wanted to help the mercenaries. He wasn't sure if it was for the right reasons, though. He would get in the way. The gun in his hand could prove more useless than the machete. Aiming. Firing. He had a few extra clips. How could he help?

He stopped in front of Akia, and because of the language barrier, pantomimed opening paper and pointing at imaginary locations.

Akia produced the map Ian had drawn.

Powell pointed at where he thought Akia's village had been. He motioned with both hands toward the path.

Another gunshot rang out. Then a short burst of rounds fired.

Akia nodded. He seemed to understand. He waved for everyone to follow him.

Powell knew that Ian said Claire should follow last. He didn't feel comfortable with that. He thought she'd be safer toward the front of the line. There was no rhyme or reason. If they were attacked, it wasn't going to make much difference where anyone stood in a line of seven people.

Rapid gunfire came from behind them. Powell kept looking back. He hoped he'd see the others running toward them. As much as he considered Marksman a bit of a thorn in his side, he was anxious to see him. No one came up behind them. He wanted to know what was happening. His imagination went a little wild. He pictured giant dinosaurs chasing the mercenaries and them firing over their shoulders at the prehistoric kaiju.

He didn't want to lose sight of Claire. She stayed close. Akia and Ruh swung machetes in an attempt to clear away the growth; the girls were directly behind Claire, side by side. They looked so young, and small, and frail; Kacancu was behind the girls, and Powell thought the young man looked anxious wanting to run on ahead, that the group might be moving too slowly for his taste.

Powell would not mind moving a little faster. No one ran, as much as walked fast. Very fast. He wasn't sure his legs had the endurance or stamina. He felt physically drained. The sweat just kept spilling from his pores. He knew his energy was being sapped. Watching his feet, he did his best not to trip. Going down and breaking a bone or twisting an ankle seemed fitting. He almost expected it to happen. It could be why no one was running too fast.

More gunshots were fired off.

Instinctively he threw his hands up, covering the back of his head.

He heard crying.

The gun play scared Mangeni. Nafula reached for the girl's hand.

There was one good thing that worked in their favor. If the mercs were really shooting at velociraptors, then he knew where the dangerous dinosaurs were. Back there. Behind them.

He wished Mangeni would stop crying. He could hear her, as if her sobs echoed, bouncing off the low-hanging leaves. He knew they were making enough noise as it was cutting their way through the trees along the path. Anything extra might be just enough to attract unwanted attention.

There were two short and two long bursts of gunfire.

It sounded a little closer to them.

Powell stopped walking and faced the sound. It came from the left, best he could tell. He took a moment to wipe at the sweat off his forehead. His forearm was already damp with sweat. All he did was merely smear it across his skin.

Kacancu tapped him on the shoulder. He spun around. The native waved him on, encouraging him to keep moving.

There was yelling. Someone screamed. They sounded like they were in severe pain. Powell didn't think his mouth could get any drier. He couldn't even swallow. His heart hammered hard behind his ribcage. He looked Kacancu in the eyes. The man looked as if fear filled him from the feet up.

"Go, go, go," Powell said, pushing Kacancu forward. They raced to catch up with the others. Kacancu's foot snagged a vine stretched across the forest floor. He pitched forward, arms out to catch himself. Powell reached for the back of Kacancu's shirt, wrapped around his waist. He managed to keep the native from falling. They didn't stop, though. They pressed on, kept moving forward. Nafula and Mangeni still held hands. They were running. Powell saw the backside of Claire, but could not see Akia and Ruh.

He worried they were all going to get separated if they didn't stay tight, close.

Ian Ross should have come with them. He would have been a better guide, a better guard.

More gunshots.

Someone was yelling, giving orders.

It sounded like Charlie Erb, that deep guttural tone of voice. That was excellent. It meant at least two of the mercenaries were still alive. Erb wouldn't be shouting commands out to himself. The voice was too muffled though. Powell couldn't hear what exactly had been said. He did realize though that the mercenaries were getting closer and closer to them. He didn't like that. Were the mercs leading the enemy right toward them?

There was too much sound. It surrounded them. It came from them. It came from every direction. Powell couldn't stop himself from looking everywhere, his neck hurt from turning this way and that. There were birds cawing. Chimps cackling. They must be in the trees, safe, watching the show unfold below them. It sounded like trees falling over. Wood splitting.

Things cracked and boomed. There was a loud explosion.

Powell saw the fiery red ball of fire roll up from between the trees and into the sky through a gap in the rain forest canopy.

Had that been a grenade that went off?

Powell tried going under a low branch. His shirt snagged onto something. He spun around. His foot hit a raised root. It was his turn to pinwheel. He realized he'd let go of the handgun as his feet left the ground. He fell hard on his side. White stars floated across blackness. Opening his eyes, the black was gone, but not the stars.

He winced, sitting up. He touched his middle finger to his temple. The skin was sliced open. Blood oozed from the gash. Other than that, he was fine. When he stood up, he wobbled. His legs felt wiry, like they might not support his weight. He set a palm against a tree for balance. He opened his eyes wide and breathed out, "Whoa," he said.

He felt woozy.

The others were gone. He couldn't even see Kacancu.

Where had he dropped the gun? It had to be in the brush to the right. He got back down onto his knees. That felt a hundred percent better than standing at the moment. He knew if he passed out now he didn't have far to fall. Passing out might just happen, too. He felt around with his hands.

And stopped. He remembered the size of the spiders. The snakes. The creatures that lived in this godforsaken land. He couldn't leave the gun. They needed the protection it offered.

He heard someone yelling for help. It was either Stacy Jennings or Becky Robinson.

She sounded close. Too close.

It wasn't Claire. That much he was certain.

He stood back up. He kicked the brush out of the way with his foot. Nothing was biting him through the steel-toe boot. At least, he didn't think anything could.

He parted aside branches and thick, fuzzy green leaves. He hoped he hadn't lost the gun.

It wasn't lost. It fell right in this area. He just wasn't sure how long he'd dedicate looking for it. At some point, Claire would realize he wasn't with them. Someone would. He didn't want them turning around and coming back for him. This was his fault. He would not be the reason for slowing them down. They had so far to go still.

But he didn't want to leave the gun.

A rifle fired off three shots. They sounded timed. Calculated. Bang. Bang. Bang.

He hoped the mercs were dropping dinosaurs, eliminating the threat once and for all. He just wanted to reach the rendezvous quickly and safely.

"Louis? Louis?"

It was Claire. They were coming back for him. Or waiting for him.

He'd have to give up on the...

He saw the gun just at the moment he was about to give up the search. He bent forward and retrieved it. His head felt like it was half-filled with water. It sloshed around freely inside his skull. It made him teeter left and right on unsteady legs. Regardless, he had the gun, and he was on his feet.

He ran toward the sound of Claire's voice. The first thing he wanted to do was tell her to stop shouting. If the mercs were close enough for them to hear, the dinosaurs would surely hear her yelling his name, too.

The danger was all around them.

What if the mercs couldn't differentiate between them running through the trees, as opposed to a velociraptor running through the trees, and just opened fire?

"Louis!" It was Kacancu. He smiled, either proud he'd said a name in English, or just to see Powell alive and still following them.

After a few more steps, and around a slight bend in the trail, were the others.

"What happened?" Claire said.

"I tripped," Powell said. "We need to keep moving."

"We weren't leaving you, Louis."

There was no arguing. He wouldn't leave her behind either. "Okay. Let's keep going."

Another grenade exploded. The black smoke was all Powell saw. Thankfully, the trees and everything in the Congo was perpetually wet. A forest fire would not help the situation any. "Come on, everyone. Let's go. Let's go!"

It felt like they were in the middle of a war zone. Powell didn't have eyes on the enemy.

They moved faster now. Almost running, they parted branches and leaves with the back of their hands as best they could. Powell was thankful it was midday. If they had been forced to move this fast in the dark, it could have been treacherous.

Ahead, a tree fell over.

It landed across the path. Akia had stopped just in time. Had he have been running any faster, he might have been crushed under the weight.

Gunfire sounded. The ka-ka-ka-ka-ka was loud. Close.

Powell and the others huddled around Akia. Ruh climbed over the trunk. Powell lifted Mangeni. She struggled in his grasp, kicking and flailing. He did not know how to calm her down. There wasn't time. He hoisted her up and over the tree. Ruh took the handoff and set her down on the ground. Nafula was next. Akia sat on the trunk and held out his hand. Claire reached for it. He lifted her up and over.

Kacancu went next, and then Powell.

What knocked the tree over?

There was a roar. It sounded like a monster from a horror movie.

"Was that what I think it was?" Powell said. He wasn't looking for an answer. He wasn't even sure if he'd spoken the words out loud.

Something exploded to their left.

The ball of fire was so close that Powell felt the heat on his arm. He watched the flames lick at the forest canopy. "We're right here!" He wanted the mercs to know where they were. He didn't want them tossing a grenade at them. "We're right here!"

He hated shouting. He didn't want the dinosaurs to know their location. He couldn't think of any other way to warn the mercs, though.

There was another growl.

It was definitely unlike anything he had ever heard before.

Akia kept waving his arms, he said something over and over, that Powell could only assume meant, "This way, this way!"

They trotted along the path again. Not running. Powell kept looking up. He didn't think falling trees was going to be an issue. Now he wanted to be ready. Anything could happen.

More gunfire.

Akia was stopped. He stood still, like a statue.

Everyone else stopped.

Powell felt the hairs on the back of his neck stand. "Why are we stopped?"

Claire held up a hand.

Ahead of them, just a few feet in front of Akia, Powell saw it. The thing blended in well with the trees. It was like natural camouflage. It was the head that moved, that gave it away.

The velociraptor stood about six or seven feet tall. Its soft grey, almost bluish flesh matched the surroundings. It reminded Powell of a chameleon. The dinosaur seemed to be trying to change color. Was that possible? Was that something they could do?

Mucus sprayed off flaring nostrils.

It must smell them. He could smell them. Their body odor was rank, raw. He hoped standing still made a difference.

The weight of the gun in Powell's hand increased. It was almost as if it wanted him to remember he was holding one. Even if he had been a skilled sniper, he wasn't sure if he'd take a shot. Not with everyone else in front of him. He had never fired a weapon. That made him more dangerous than the velociraptor.

His mind was blank. Black. There was not a single helpful thought inside his brain. His legs felt like they'd been coated in cement. He couldn't move. He hadn't tried moving. He just knew if he wanted to, there would be no way his legs would respond.

Claire was too close to the dinosaur.

That was the one thought that made its way into his mind.

Claire was too close.

He couldn't keep still. He needed to do something. The forest had grown deathly silent. Except for everyone breathing, there was nothing else to hear. Even at a whisper, it sounded like he was screaming. The dinosaur continued to sniff the air, its head slowly pivoting left and right. He felt the rubber grip on the handgun handle. He let his first finger slide into the guard and set it softly on the trigger. He made sure every movement was slow. Cautious.

Time both stopped and sped up. He felt like he was moving in slow motion. It seemed like they'd been frozen in place for hours.

A mosquito dared land on his neck. The proboscis stung as it punctured his skin. The bugs in the Congo were giant compared to the itty bitty things back home. He almost slapped at the insect filling its belly with his blood, but refrained.

He was going to have to take the shot. It's what Marksman would have done. Point, aim—keep both eyes open—and shoot. He could do it.

He had to do it.

He needed to do something.

Inside his head, he counted down. Three. Two. One. . .

Powell heard a gunshot. The velociraptor's head bounced back on its neck. A hole was in the center of its head. Blood oozed from the wound. It opened its mouth, revealing rows of sharp teeth. Powell expected the beast to scream. No sound came out of it. Instead, it fell forward. It's tiny front arms, with bowed talons, did nothing to break the fall. It went down hard. Its body crumbled to the ground in a heap.

Trees shook. Branches parted. John Marksman stepped onto the path. "Is everyone okay?" he said.

Something was coming up fast behind them.

Powell felt renewed. He pivoted and raised his weapon.

Stacy Jennings came at him. "Lower your weapon," she said, aiming her rifle at him.

Powell realized he was holding his breath. He exhaled and dropped his arm to his side. The nightmare was far from over, but he couldn't help but feel a little hopeful. "Where are the others?"

"It's just us," Stacy said. She lowered her rifle and walked past Powell.

"Ian?" Claire said. "He went back into the jungle looking for all of you. Did you see Ian?"

Marksman and Stacy looked at each other.

"We didn't see him," Marksman said.

Powell noticed that Marksman's pants were ripped open along the thigh. A gash in his leg was visible. He was bleeding, but not profusely. There were cuts on his forearms and a slash under his left eye that went from his ear to the bridge of his nose.

"We can't leave him behind," Powell said. "We're not just going to leave without him, are we? And I heard Charlie. I know I heard Charlie Erb not that long ago."

"Where are you headed?" Marksman said, as if Powell had not spoken at all.

"We're dropping them off at a village and then continuing for the river," Claire said.

"Okay. Let's keep moving then." Marksman checked the ammunition in his rifle. He seemed satisfied. He retrieved a bandana from one of his pockets and tied it around his thigh, pulling tight on the ends. He lifted his rifle slightly in his hands, ready to fire at anything he didn't like. He appeared ready, or as ready as possible under the circumstances.

"But, but Erb and Ian?" Powell said.

"Charlie's dead," Stacy said. She didn't look much better off than Marksman. She had cuts on her face and forehead. Her right sleeve was shredded. She had three lacerations across her forearm, as if something sharp swiped at her, and she'd thrown her arm up in defense. "I never saw Ian. If he was back there somewhere, he can't be alive."

"Did Ian know the plan? Was he going to meet with you at the river?" Marksman said.

"Yes, he was," Powell said.

"Then that's where we'll find him if he's still alive. There's no point going backwards. We need to keep going forward," Marksman said. "He's well-trained. If he couldn't find us, he'd head that way. The river."

It made sense, Powell thought. He hoped Marksman was right. He wanted Ian to be alive.

Everyone began walking forward. Powell saw Stacy limped, favoring her left leg. It might be a sprained ankle, or broken bone.

Powell stopped at the dropped velociraptor corpse. He looked down at the body. It was so big. Not at all what he expected. The skin that had once looked greyish blue, now was puke green with light brown tiger stripes. Its eyes were still open and were about the size of his palm. He couldn't look away from the talons. They looked like long bone daggers. They would easily rip apart flesh.

Stepping over the dinosaur, Powell looked back. They hadn't made it very far. Time was against them. He wondered how many raptors were dead, how many had Marksman and the other mercs killed?

Most of all, Powell wondered, how long would it be before the sun set, and how many more raptors were still alive and stalking them?

CHAPTER 16

John Marksman let Akia and Ruh lead the way. They swung machetes with skill. The long, sharpened blades sliced through the branches, hacked through the leaves and cleared the path cleanly.

Powell held his handgun in one hand, his finger so close to the trigger. He felt far more confident with Marksman and Stacy in the group. It was hard not to. It took some of the pressure off, lightened the responsibility some. Who was he kidding? He never wanted to be in charge.

They weren't moving fast, but they *were* making pretty good progress. If velociraptors followed them, the animals kept their distance. It didn't stop Powell from scanning the brush. Everything looked like it might be a predator. He knew his mind played tricks on him. The heat, humidity, and the pressure overwhelmed him. It took tremendous effort to put one leg in front of the other. It was almost mechanical, reflex. He knew if he were alone, there was a good chance he'd never survive.

Powell remembered when he was young and in his bedroom, and he'd hear a noise. It always sounded like it came from either the closet or the darkest corner of the room. His mother never let him sleep with a light on. His curtains were always drawn closed. The light switch was by the door, at least twelve feet away from his bed. Any other boy might brave the distance and make a break for the switch. Throwing light over the darkness would surely reveal nothing sinister in the room. Not him. Powell chose to pull the bedspread over his head. He'd cry, keeping his sobs as silent as possible. He wanted to close his eyes against his fears, but couldn't. For hours he would lie in bed, shaking, waiting for whatever lurked in the closet, or the darkest corner, to come and devour him. It never happened. Eventually, he'd fall asleep. The point was, he didn't fight. He didn't face his fear. He hid under a blanket.

Without the mercenaries beside him now, he feared it wouldn't be long before he reverted to his childhood ways. That scared him the most.

The rain started coming down. Not hard. It was a mist that almost hung floating in the air. It was like he could part the moisture with the wave from the back of his hand.

A gunshot rang out. It could have come from behind them. Everyone stopped walking, on sudden alert from the sound.

Powell shook his head. "I thought you said the others were dead?"

Stacy and Marksman exchanged looks. Powell couldn't read it clearly.

"Were the others dead or *not*?" Powell said.

"I saw Charlie go. The raptor was hiding beneath leaves. It was so quiet. I was a few feet behind him. I never saw it there, waiting. And then all at once it sprang forward. It's mouth was so much larger than I expected. It bit down on Charlie's neck. There was so much blood. He didn't have time to scream," Stacy said.

"He wouldn't have screamed," Marksman said. It wasn't meant as a contradiction, just a clarification that perhaps defined the kind of soldier Charlie Erb was.

"And Becky?" Claire said.

"There were two of them. She was against a tree. She'd either run out of ammunition, or couldn't reload. She looked terrified," Marksman said, staring at the ground. "I couldn't get the shot. They were right in front of her. Their talons kept moving, and clicking together, and it was like they were smiling. I swear, it looked like they smiled, enjoying her fear. She's dead. I saw her die. And then I shredded them. My ammo cut them to pieces."

"Ian?" Powell said. "Who saw him die?"

Stacy and Marksman looked at each other again. They didn't move their heads. Their eyes just found each other.

"That's him back there," Powell said.

"Stay here," Marksman said. "No one moves unless you have to. Otherwise, give me five minutes, and then get out of here. Meet at the river like planned. Find a boat and get on the water and we'll catch up with you there. Five minutes," he said, and looked at Stacy, "not a second more. Understood?"

She nodded. "Hurry."

Marksman ran through the trees. Powell lost sight of the man after only a few steps. It was almost as if Marksman were a magician who had just passed through a solid wall.

Five minutes would feel like an eternity. "We should have some water," Powell said. He knew the supplies they carried were limited. He took bottles from his backpack and passed them around. He set the backpack down on the ground and sat on it.

He wished he had some concept of time. It felt as if hours had passed by. They might have.

His legs were weak and rubbery. Getting up in five minutes might prove harder than expected. His body was sore. Had been since the initial hike from the SUV.

"How are you, Claire?" Powell needed a distraction.

She shook her head, but was smiling. "I don't feel like this is happening, that it could really be happening."

He set his hand on her shoulder. She didn't shrug it off. Instead, she touched his hand with her fingers.

"We're getting out of here," he said. It was an empty promise. He wasn't fooling her. The way things looked, he didn't believe it either. It was something to say, something that needed saying.

"Hopefully we're close to one of the villages. If we can at least get these people home..."

"We need to let them loose. We have ourselves to worry about," Stacy said.

"I'm not having this conversation again," Powell said.

"I'm just saying. This is their home. They know the land. They have ways of dealing with the dinosaurs," the merc said.

Powell looked at the natives. Each of them seemed to watch the exchange. "If they thought they were safer on their own, don't you think they would have taken off? They're just as frightened as the rest of us."

"They're just kids," Claire added. "Teenagers. Hell, not even!"

Stacy pursed her lips. "I learned one thing over the years. A job is a job. At the end of the day, though, it's about me. It has to be about me. If I get killed out here, who is going to care?"

"I would care," Claire said.

Stacy shook her head. "You don't even know me. You don't know any of us."

The tension was thick. Powell held out his hands, a calming gesture that didn't seem to diffuse a single thing. "Look, the villages are on the way. We have the map."

More gunshots sounded behind them.

Stacy gripped her rifle. She looked toward the trees, and then at the path. "Come on. We're moving."

"It hasn't been five minutes," Powell said.

She waved them forward with the barrel of the rifle. "We're going. Let's go, let's go."

Powell stood up, put on his backpack. He wasn't comfortable with this. "We should wait."

"But we're not," Stacy said. "John knows where we'll be. Look, you haven't seen these things. They're vicious. They're relentless. They're—"

It crashed through the trees.

Powell stood still, staring. His jaw dropped, mouth wide open.

The velociraptor had black eyes. Its skin was dark, grey. It let out a roar as it stepped onto the path. Its voice vibrated, rattling around inside its throat. The red tongue shot forward as if trying to escape the thing's mouth. Thick, white saliva dripped from the row of top teeth. It stood up tall, tiny arms outstretched, talons barred.

He almost laughed. His mind had done a complete one-eighty. Despite everyone talking about dinosaurs, he'd accepted their word as truth, but until now, until this very moment, he didn't believe it.

Stacy stumbled backwards. A rock on the ground tripped her. She fell backward. Her ass hit the mud. Bullets went flying. Fire burst from the muzzle with each rapid shot. Nothing came close to hitting the raptor.

The young girls were screaming. They hugged each other. Their faces were pressed tight together, cheek to cheek. The three young men took steps backward, toward Powell, as if they forgot about the machetes they held in their hands.

A machete seemed like little more than a pocket knife at this point.

Stacy aimed the rifle at the dinosaur. Her hair flopped in front of her face, partially covering her eyes.

Powell could peripherally see Claire, but didn't want to turn away. He couldn't look away.

He was a frozen statue.

Frozen.

He was a child again, a young boy in his dark bedroom hiding under blankets so the monsters might think he was someplace else.

The velociraptor was fast, stepping on Stacy's leg with a three-toed foot. The talons on the toes spiked through her thigh. Blood spurted from the wound. Stacy lost her grip on the rifle. Her head went back as she opened her mouth to scream. She never had the chance. The raptor drove its head forward, teeth bared, and bit into Stacy's face. From where Powell stood, he heard the crunch of bone as Stacy's head was crushed between the raptor's jaws.

The raptor set the other leg on Stacy's chest. It pushed against her body, as it lifted its head, ripping Stacy's head off of her shoulders. A string of spine came out of her back and was still attached to the back of the skull. Blood and flesh, muscle and torn meat dripped off the severed vertebrae along with dangling strands of sinew and bone.

Powell remembered his gun. It was too late for Stacy, but he remembered it. He took aim. It was a clear shot. He kept both eyes open, with both hands on the grip. He tried to keep the handgun steady. He felt like he was aiming directly for the raptor's head. He pulled the trigger. The gun kicked a little in his hand. It was far louder than he'd expected. The raptor didn't look hurt. It chewed on Stacy's head. White bone and bloody meat fell out of its mouth as it chewed, and then slowly it turned and looked directly at him.

It was like it *knew* Powell meant it harm, that Powell was actually a danger to it.

It spat Stacy from its mouth and walked over what was left of her body.

The young girls shrieked. Claire pulled them out of the way. It looked like they'd disappeared into the woods. It felt like everyone was gone. There was just the raptor...and him. They were the only two living, breathing things on the path. Powell never lowered the handgun. He let off another shot.

The bullet nicked the raptor's shoulder. It stopped and stood up tall. When it roared, that tongue flapped around inside its mouth. The thing's face was covered in blood. Stacy's blood.

Powell shot at it again.

This time he'd hit it. A hole was in its neck, just above what might be considered the collarbone. Blood oozed out of the wound.

The rain came down harder. It wasn't a heavy deluge, but it was raining good.

Powell had nowhere to go. He needed to stand his ground. He was right, the others were gone. They hid in the thicket. They were safe.

He was not going to stay under the blanket and hope everything worked out. Powell dropped one of his arms to his side. He raised the handgun a little higher. He stood sideways, aiming.

The raptor took a step toward him.

Then another.

Powell had no idea how many rounds were loaded inside the weapon. He couldn't recall how many times he fired the gun. There wasn't any time to check. He thought he'd fired once, maybe twice. Three times would have been the most. He'd missed. He'd nicked it. He'd hit it in the throat. Three times.

The guttural noises coming out of the raptor's mouth completely unnerved him. He knew his arm trembled, his hand shook, and his aim was for shit. It was why he waited. He might not know how many rounds were left but he knew there at least had to be one left. At the very least.

The closer the thing got, the bigger his target. It would be harder to miss.

If he didn't kill it, though, he was as good as dead.

Dead might be fine.

Dying the way Stacy just died was not. He could not fathom the pain she felt. He did not want to get eaten.

It took another step.

A gunshot erupted from the trees.

Claire. She used one of her bullets. She hit it, too. She hit the raptor, but hadn't killed it. It stopped approaching, but only long enough to scan the trees.

Shit, he thought. "Here I am!"

He didn't want the thing going after Claire and the young girls. He wanted them safe. He was doing this—taking a stand against a prehistoric reptile and fighting childhood fears so they would all be safe. "Over here!"

The raptor's head snapped forward. Its dilated eyes locked on him.

Thunder boomed from unseen clouds above the forest canopy.

They didn't need another storm. They didn't need another hurdle to overcome. Everything was against them. Nothing worked with them. They needed some luck. A splash of luck, a touch of hope to hold onto.

The raptor ran at him.

There wasn't much gap between them.

Powell counted off two seconds and then fired, pulling the trigger once, twice, three times.

The bullets grouped on the raptor's sloped forehead. He worried they might have ricocheted off the crocodile like skin. Until the raptor just fell forward. Its chin slammed hard on the soft ground. The thing never looked away from Powell, though. Not until thin eyelids fluttered and closed over black eyeballs.

Powell didn't want to go anywhere near it. He'd seen enough horror movies in his youth. The hand always shot forward and grabbed onto the lone survivor's leg at the very end. Only, this wasn't a movie. The raptor didn't have a hand. Powell wasn't a lone survivor, and this was far from the end of the story.

CHAPTER 17

"It's dead," Louis Powell said. He kicked at the raptor's head with the toe of his boot. He spoke quietly, hoping those hiding in the trees and bushes heard him. He didn't want to yell. If the raptors hunted in packs, then it was likely more were nearby. He couldn't recall the last time he'd heard gunshots from either Marksman or Ian Ross. He wanted to believe they were still alive, on the run, and headed for the river, too.

Claire emerged from the forest first. "Louis?"

"It's okay. I'm okay," he said. Everything had happened so fast. He wasn't sure he could recall all of the events. He was confident his dreams would be plagued. Nightmares were going to prevent him from getting a solid sleep ever again.

"I tried to help you. I tried to kill it," she said. She was trembling. Her lower lip quivered. Claire kept one arm behind her back. Powell saw the young girls behind her. They clung to Claire's shirt and peered around her back.

He nodded. "Thank you. You did. You helped me," he said. He wanted to spend some time reassuring her and make sure she was okay. He wished there was time, but there wasn't. "Get the others. We need to keep moving."

The rain came down steadier than before. It fell in large drops, as if the rain had pooled on the canopy and was now draining down from the heavy leaves. The rainwater felt somewhat refreshing. It took some of the bite out of the humidity, cleaned some of the dirt and sweat and stink off his body. That was the only silver lining Powell could find at the moment. He grabbed it and hung onto it, because at least it was *something*.

The young men stepped onto the path, heads hung low. Powell thought he could imagine the thoughts passing through their minds. They had taken off, practically dove into the bushes when everything went down. They looked ashamed, as if they felt guilty.

He wished they didn't feel that way. They were not cowards. This was not a normal situation. He clapped Akia on the back, gave him a quick rub. He wished he knew French. He desperately wanted to communicate with each of them. All he could do was point ahead and motion with his hand that he wanted them to begin moving again.

Akia understood. He readied his machete. Ruh stood by his side.

Powell checked the ammunition in his gun. Best he could tell he had two bullets left. Two. Claire had fired one shot. They were very low on ammo. He felt like a thief, but his actions couldn't be helped.

Leaning over Stacy's shredded corpse, Powell retrieved her rifle. He pulled off her vest. Affixed to it were pockets with clips of extra ammo and two grenades. Her body was ripe. He saw chunks of missing flesh and tissue. He put on the vest. She had a handgun in a holster on her hip. He closed his eyes and cringed as he unfastened the belt and slid it off her waist. He clipped it on around his, doing his best to ignore the warm, wet blood that now coated his palms and fingers.

At least they were more heavily armed than before.

The seven of them cut a way through the forest, staying on the path. Powell only hoped they were close to a village.

The daylight was being spent quickly. Too much time was passing by, and it felt like they'd barely made it anywhere. He ignored the thought in his brain that insisted they had just been going around and round in circles. He knew they weren't. Fear that bad luck followed him everywhere kept him from believing it though.

The natives knew where they were going. Stacy had been right about that. This was their home. The trails were in their backyards. If they were uselessly going in circles, Akia, or Ruh, or Kacancu would know.

In fact Akia bounced up and down, waving them on. "Par ici! Par ici!"

Claire raised an eyebrow.

"I think he wants us to follow him," Powell said. He saw no reason why they shouldn't. He said, "Par ici, par ici!"

Akia nodded, smiling. It was the first time Powell could recall seeing the young man smile. He stepped off the path, cutting a way deeper into the forest. Claire reached out and touched Powell's arm.

"Where is he taking us?" Claire asked. "This can't be a good idea?"

Powell whispered. "Let's just follow him. They know these woods. We don't. We're alone now. Us. You. Me. We need to trust these guys to help us."

They stepped over raised roots and around mossy growths. No telling what might be hiding underneath. Powell was as careful as he could be to step on only ground he could see. His phobias increased the deeper they journeyed away from the path. Why he'd felt even moderately safe on some worn trail was ridiculous. But he did. And now that they were off it, everything had changed. It suddenly seemed like the rain forest felt the exact same way. The more they walked, the more alive everything around them became. Powell heard more animal calls than he could ever identify. The chatter came from above them and from all four sides. It might not be vicious velociraptors stalking them at that very moment, but they were being watched.

That was Powell's last thought before he heard it.

It was the reverberating roar of a raptor, or two. The sound was worse than nails scratching down a chalkboard. It was cliché, but the best Powell could come up with. A shiver raced from the top of his head down his spine. His legs went weak and his hand shook. He had the rifle now, which should have provided some solace, or consolation. He had no idea what to do with the rifle though. He'd gotten a fast lesson on how to use the handgun.

"Run!" Powell shouted. It was not needed. They'd all heard the raptor behind them.

He turned the assault rifle over in his hands. The trigger. He'd seen Marksman remove the curved, rectangular cartridge in front of the trigger. He almost dropped the rifle as he leapt over raised roots. He managed to hold onto the rifle and keep his balance.

His finger found a release switch. He pulled out the cartridge. There were bullets inside. He had no idea how many. He shoved the clip back into the slot. It locked in place.

He realized he could hear the raptors closing in behind him.

Their feet crushed branches under foot. It sounded like they were ramming their heads into trees, knocking things over. There was no way he was looking back. If he did he'd trip, fall, and get devoured. There were far too many obstacles and hurdles. Every running step he took demanded his attention.

The others were not having much more success. Claire was concentrating on the young girls. She kept them ahead of her. If anything, they were better at running through the rainforest than Claire was. The young men were far, far ahead. They ran like the wind. The leapt over bushes, ducked under branches, and easily swerved around trees.

Powell needed some kind of plan. The raptors would overtake him any moment. They were so close he thought he could feel their breath on the back of his neck. If he cut left, or right and averted an attack, all he would do is make Claire and the young girls more susceptible.

He aimed the rifle into the air. He let his finger squeeze the trigger. Bullets shot toward the top of the canopy. He had to take his finger off the trigger fast, or risk using all of the ammunition. This rifle was not a semi-automatic, but an actual machine gun.

He knew what he had to do. If he thought too much about it, he'd chicken out.

Instead of dwelling, he acted. Without slowing down, he threw himself forward. Tucking in his head, he somersaulted around. He wound up sitting on one leg, with the other foot planted on the ground. He didn't have time to aim. He squeezed the trigger and fired.

Although he knew the raptor had been on his heels, he didn't realize just how close he had been to getting chomped on.

The rounds tore into the beast's flesh. Caught off guard, the raptor ran right through Powell. The weight of its chest barrelled Powell over. He was splayed out on his back. The raptor stepped onto his gut. A talon slashed through his shirt and into his skin. The assault rifle was knocked out of his hands.

Powell slapped a hand over his stomach. He was bleeding, and the laceration burned. A heat ran through the inside of his body. He winced as he rolled onto his side. His arm stretched out for the rifle.

The raptor stopped chasing the others. It had its target now. Powell was the bleeding meat attracting its attention.

Instead of looking to see where the rifle was exactly, he kept looking at the turned around raptor. It seemed to study him. It snorted out of both nostrils.

Powell knew more than one raptor had been chasing them. He wondered where the others had gone. Claire and everyone else were still in danger.

He lunged for the weapon, grunting. It felt like his guts were spilling out of the gash in his belly. They weren't. He didn't even think the stab from the talon was that deep. It just hurt like a motherfucker.

Staying on his stomach, Powell gripped the rifle as best he could, and took aim just as the raptor charged forward. It opened its mouth wide. Thick gooey saliva dripped off the top row of teeth and spilled over the lower lip. With everything there was to eat in the Congo, Powell couldn't help wondering why this particular prehistoric monster looked so damned hungry.

The machine gun let out a *cha-cha-cha-cha-cha-cha* of rapid firing. Powell thought most of the bullets missed the raptor. He saw large green leaves shredded and tree bark fly as the tree splintered in long shards. Time moved fast. Not slow. Everything he wanted to do needed to happen all at once. He kept both eyes open and focused on the target as best he could. The raptor was almost on him.

He aimed for the mouth. It was open. It looked like the best target. It seemed like the bullets did little to the thick lizard-like skin. He kept the bursts of gunfire short. He was aware of limited ammo. He knew he'd grabbed additional cartridges off Stacy, but the last thing he wanted to do right now was reload. Holy shit, he couldn't imagine having to do that for the first time with a dinosaur about to pounce on him. He wasn't trained for this kind of shit.

A bullet struck the velociraptor under the jaw. It plunged through the tongue and slammed into the roof of the mouth. That didn't drop the beast, but it stopped him. The raptor shook its head, as if a child stung by a wasp. The raptor danced around.

Powell was watching, instead of reacting. It took him a moment. If this raptor could shake off a gunshot through the mouth, he was in trouble. He got to a knee, ignoring the pain in his stomach, and fired at the injured raptor.

The rounds hit home. Chunks of raptor flesh were carved off its body. It bled from the new holes. The damned thing wouldn't fall, though. It looked toward the sky and roared. Countless bullet holes ripped through its body, and all Powell had done was manage to piss it off.

The raptor regained a sense of composure. It lowered its snout and locked its eyes on its prey.

Powell squeezed the trigger. Bullets sailed out of the barrel, flame and smoke left behind, and slammed into the raptor. The dinosaur took a step back, and then another, and a third before it fell to the side. Its hole-pierced tongue dangled out of the side of its mouth. The short arms twitched, the talons raked at nothing but air.

The trigger was still squeezed.

The rifle was still aimed at the raptor.

The bullet supply had run out at some point.

Eventually Powell relaxed his grip. He ejected the spent cartridge and locked in its place a new one. He found it difficult to stand. He stayed on one knee for a moment and listened to the forest. If the others were still being chased, he'd have to find them.

Looking behind him, Powell half expected to see more raptors running toward him.

There weren't any.

They had to be around though. There had to be more.

CHAPTER 18

Louis Powell got to his feet slowly, a hand draped over his wound. He was not worried about bleeding out. The fear of an infection is what nearly paralysed him. He trudged forward, past the fallen raptor. After a little bit, he began jogging. He heard his breathing inside his head, behind his ears. Huffing and puffing as he picked up speed.

There was no path to follow. The best he could do is head toward where he'd last seen anyone.

"Louis!"

Powell stopped and looked around.

"Up here!"

Claire and the girls were in a tree. Powell sighed. At least they were safe. Climbing a tree made sense. The only problem was it didn't get you anywhere except stuck. He waved them down and used the rifle strap to keep the gun slung over his shoulder as he helped Mangeni and Nafula out of the tree, and then Claire.

"I thought..." Claire didn't finish her sentence. There was no need. Powell knew what she was going to say.

"It's okay. We're okay," he said. He almost added, *for now*, but didn't. She knew that much to be true. "Where are the boys?"

"They kept running. They didn't look back once," Claire said. There was an accusatory tone to her voice. Powell let it slide. He still wasn't upset with the young men for hiding, or for running.

"I'm kind of turned around out here. Maybe leaving the path wasn't such a good idea," Powell said.

"You're hurt?"

"I'm okay. It's nothing," Powell said.

Nafula tugged on Claire's shirt, and then pointed.

Powell sighed. He no longer felt confident following native directions. They needed to reach the river. They needed to get out of the jungle. It was no different now than it had been earlier. They knew the forest. Following their lead still made more sense. He knelt down in front of the girl. "Your home is that way?"

She just looked at him.

He stood up. "We might as well see where they take us."

At some point on their trek, the rain stopped. Powell realized it, but couldn't recall exactly when the rain had stopped. He almost missed it. The heat and humidity crept back in. He would never complain about New York weather again.

They came to a clearing. Trees had been removed. Through the thinning of trunks, Powell saw long rectangular structures. He almost cried. They'd made it to a village.

Nafula took Claire's hand and said something to Mangeni, and then Mangeni took Powell's hand.

They left the thicket of the forest and entered the village. People stopped what they were doing and stared.

A woman shouted and ran at them. She cried as she dropped to her knees. Mangeni let go of Powell's hand and ran to her mother. The two embraced.

Ruh came out of a building. He made eye contact with Powell, and then turned around and went back inside.

Nafula smiled and waved hello to people. She spoke quickly, perhaps telling them about the last two days.

Mangeni reached for Powell's hand again, and then pulled on his arm as they followed behind Claire and Nafula.

The natives wore what looked like American clothing. They were in slacks and jeans, dress shirts and t-shirts. They wore boots or running shoes. They turned spits with cooking meat over open flames and ground grains by hand in large ceramic bowls. All eyes were on Powell and Claire, though.

Ruh came back out of the building with an older man behind him. Ruh pointed at them and the young girls brought Powell and Claire over.

"You have braved the K-Rex to save our family," the older man said. The English was broken, but clear enough for Powell to understand.

Powell assumed the older man was some kind of tribal leader. He really had no idea. Best he could do was try and call on his memory from watching National Geographic as a kid. Either way he supposed it didn't matter. The man spoke English, and hopefully he wanted to help them.

"We are trying to get to the river," Powell said.

The older man had smooth skin. It was difficult to judge his age. He wore a red shirt tucked into khaki-colored slacks, held up with a black leather belt. His feet were bare, and long toenails scratched at the muddy earth. "You are safe in the village."

"Thank you," Powell said. "Thank you. We appreciate that. We do. But we need to make it to the river, east of here. I think it is east of here."

"The river. Yes. But it is getting late. You will never make it there in time. It is a long ways away. Stay here tonight. Eat with us. Sleep in a bed. In the morning, I will give you directions to the river," the older man said.

"Will someone be able to guide us? You know, take us to the river?" Powell said. He noticed the other villagers were closing in on them. It probably wasn't every day they saw a man and woman from America. He supposed it wasn't often that the natives saw white people.

Smaller children ran in circles, giggling and singing. Whenever Powell looked at one of them, they would laugh uncontrollably and cover their mouth with their hands.

The old man shook his head. "Ah, no."

Powell smiled, cocking his head to one side, a little confused. "No?" This time Powell spoke a little slower, and just a little louder. "Maybe you don't understand. We need someone to lead the way. We will follow them. Or else we might not make it to the river."

"No. It is you that does not understand. In the morning, I will give you very clear directions. If you cannot follow them, then you do not deserve to find the river. I am not letting any of my people out of the village for a while. The K-Rex are very," he paused, his hand rolled around at the wrist as if searching for the right word, and then said, "agitated. Come. Let's have something to eat."

# # #

Powell and Claire shared a bed. There was nothing romantic about it. Mangeni and her younger sister slept in the bed next to them. There were no walls inside the house. Blankets on string strung from one wall to the next are what separated the rooms. Mangeni's father snored. It sounded like a train, breaking down. The man's nose rumbled and roared, and then whined and whistled.

"Do you think Marksman found Ian?" Claire said.

"I don't know."

"Do you think they already made it to the river?"

"I don't know."

"Would they leave without us?" she said.

"I'm not sure. I don't know."

"I mean if they reached the river first, they might assume we died, that the dinosaurs ate us or something. How long are they supposed to wait for us? It's not like they're just going to stand around hoping we show up. They probably don't care one way or the other if we show up. You saw them? You saw how you practically had to twist John's arm off to get him to go back and look for Ian. And Ian was—is, Ian is —his friend."

"Shh," Powell said. He attempted combing a finger through her hair. It wasn't simple. Dried mud made it nearly impossible. Instead, he petted the top of her head. "Shh. You are worrying too much about things that we can't change."

"What is that supposed to mean?" she said.

"If they left without us, the plan is still the same. Find a boat, follow the river until we reach a city. We just have to get out of the jungle, and away from the raptors, because apparently, we've agitated them," he said.

She laughed.

"That's funny?"

She nodded. "Yes. It is."

He hugged her head to his chest. The night had just started. If his dreams were nightmare free, he'd close his eyes. He was too afraid to risk it, though. So instead he stayed awake.

CHAPTER 19

Powell guessed it was either the village shaman or a witch doctor that made a ceremony out of starting leaves on fire and then fanning the smoke over his and Claire's bodies. The shaman chanted while he circled them. The smoke was thick and burned Powell's throat.

"This will tell the K-Rex that you are one of us," the tribal leader explained.

"It will keep us safe?" Claire said.

"That question is not mine to answer. It will tell the K-Rex that you both are one of us. Whether he wants to eat you or not is up to him," the tribal leader said. He smiled, but there was nothing comforting about the gesture. "You are welcome to stay with us for as long as you would like."

It was a tempting offer. Powell glanced at Claire. She was looking at him. She didn't indicate a preference, but seemed to want him to decide. How long could they stay in a village in the Congo? Eventually they would have to leave. Or, eventually, someone would come looking for them.

The offer was tempting indeed. Powell held out his hand. "Thank you for your hospitality, for the water, and for the directions, but we are going to make it to the river." The leader had given each of them each a waterskin filled with what the natives considered clean drinking water—Powell refused to think about the parasites waiting to be ingested—

and just a little food in a sack. "You have been very generous."

The tribal leader shook Powell's hand. "I wish both you luck and best wishes."

Powell put a hand on Claire's shoulder and turned her around. They started walking toward the edge of the village, but stopped when they heard two little voices calling out after them.

They faced the villagers. Both Mangeni and Nafula ran toward them, arms opened wide. The four of them hugged. Powell was surprised at how the goodbye hit him. He'd barely spoken to the kids. He knew it was guilt that guided him. He wondered if Gary Brunson was aware of the ages of the laborers, or if he was, did he even care?

Powell looked over the faces of the villagers. He expected to see Ruh and was disappointed when he could not find him in the small gathered crowd.

"Come on," he said to Claire, "let's not waste any daylight."

# # #

"You understand where we're going?" Claire said.

The tribal leader's directions weren't so much on a map as they were a finger point. He'd said, "Go this way, and you will reach the river. Whether you stumble a little left, or stumble a little right, you will reach the river."

"We go this way," Powell said, and pointed.

"Come, come," a man said behind them.

Powell spun around with his rifle raised. "Ruh!"

Ruhakana waved for them to follow him. He ran past them, and on ahead, looking back only once to shout, "Come, come!"

"Their leader isn't going to like this," Claire said.

Powell shrugged. "Too late to worry about it now!"

Without the young girls to look after, they were able to run more swiftly, more quickly. It almost felt freeing. And besides, they hadn't seen a velociraptor since yesterday. The sun was rising in what appeared a cloudless sky. They might even make it the day without too much rain.

The heat hung on. With everything else going in their favor, Powell wasn't going to let some stifling hot air spoil the growing list of positives.

He jumped over roots and cut left around a tree. His boots were tied tight. He wasn't going to let snakes and spiders work their way into his mind. Not today.

Ruh was fast. He almost floated over the brush. It was difficult keeping up, but Powell was up to the challenge. They had to be making good time. He wasn't sure how long they had been running. Twice they had stopped to sip some water.

"What are we going to do if we don't make it to the river by morning?" Claire said, after lowering the waterskin from her mouth and brushing her forearm across her lips.

Powell looked around. "I was wondering about that myself. We can't think that way. We have to make it to the river before nightfall. I think at the pace Ruh's set, we should be okay."

At the mention of his name, Ruh smiled at them.

Powell felt so inept. He wished they could communicate. When he got back to the states, he thought about learning some other languages. Even with the six years of Spanish he took during high school and college, he still didn't feel comfortable doing more than ordering cheese and nachos with a margarita.

Ruh pressed his hand over his mouth.

Claire laughed. "What is he doing?"

Powell shook his head. "I don't know."

Ruh's eyes opened wider. He removed his hand, and then clapped it over his mouth again, nodding at them.

"I wish I knew what—"

Powell grabbed Claire's arm, silencing her. He whispered, "He's telling us to shut up. Something must be out there."

CHAPTER 20

Powell let himself believe too many times that everything was going to be all right. It might have been a simple mind trick that kept his body from shutting down. He needed a way out of la-la land. The fact that a velociraptor was stalking them helped speed up the process of change.

He held onto the rifle with both hands, ready to fire at anything that moved. Three hundred and sixty degrees was a lot of area to cover by himself. He was the only one with the rifle. Claire had her handgun, but there were only a few bullets left. Powell looked at Ruh for direction, because he sure as shit hadn't heard a single sound. He wasn't surprised. His make-believe world probably blocked out any unwanted noises.

Ruh pointed.

The raptor was behind them. At least it wasn't blocking their path forward, the way toward the river.

"The smoke, it will keep the dinosaurs away?" Claire said. Her lips quivered.

"We're fine," Powell said. "Shhh."

"Should we run?"

Running made so much sense. It was the easiest thing to do. Those things were fast. Deadly, and fast. There was no way to outrun them. If they tried taking off, it would bear down on them in seconds.

Branches snapped. *That* Powell heard.

Ruh waved his arms around to get their attention. When Powell noticed, Ruh pointed up.

It was the best first option. "Climb the tree, Claire."

"What?"

"Come on, let's go. Up, up." Powell stood by a trunk. He laced his hands together.

More branches were crunched under the weight of what had to be a raptor.

And then more. Claire stared off in that direction.

"Claire! Let's go!" He leaned forward, hands out, so she could step into them for a boost upward. Out of the corner of his eye he saw Ruh scaling a tree like a fucking squirrel. "Claire!"

She snapped back. Her lips were drawn down in a frown, eyes tearing up. "Louis," she said.

"Get over here. Climb, climb!"

Claire stepped into Powell's hands. She set her hands onto the back of his head for balance. He counted off three and bounced her up several feet. She reached for branches and pulled herself up, her feet searching for traction on the bark.

The sounds got closer. More frequent. Without seeing it, Powell thought it sounded like the raptor was now running at them.

"Give me your hand," Claire said.

The siren of the raptor's roar killed the silence inside the forest.

"Keep climbing. Get as high up as Ruh," Powell said. "Go!"

He jumped then, his hand grasping onto a branch. It cracked and broke off from the rest of the tree. Powell hadn't expected it. He fell. It wasn't far, but he wasn't ready. He crashed onto his back.

"Get up!" Claire yelled.

Powell looked to his left.

The beast ran at him. That was motivation. Powell rolled onto his knees, got to his feet and was running in one, or nearly one, fluid motion. His eyes searched for more low branches. There had to be a tree he could climb.

The raptor let out another roar. It made Powell think of old movies, as if the roar was a battle cry. A trumpet signalling the start of war.

He watched the ground while he ran and kept his footing as best he could. Best he could tell, he was still headed in the right direction, toward the river, but away from Claire and Ruh. He chanced a look back.

There were two raptors. Two. They ran at him side by side. Powell thought his heart stopped beating. It felt like it swelled inside his chest and would soon explode.

And then, bam!

He was falling, had tripped over a snaking vine. He went down hard. He thought his elbow cracked. It had crashed onto a rock. The throbbing that shot up his arm to his shoulder and down to his fingertips made him suspect he'd shattered bone. His whole arm tingled. He had no clue how such a spot could be nicknamed the funny bone, except that he almost found himself giggling from the pain. Shit—was that why?

The two raptors bumped into each other. It wasn't a clumsy move. The motion seemed almost human, *sophomoric*. When they each roared, Powell imagined them like two fat drunk guys who hadn't eaten in days and were stepping up to a buffet of their favorite foods.

Powell was lying on the rifle. He struggled rolling around, hands behind his back, and on the shoulder strap.

He wasn't going to make it. They were steps away.

Louis Powell did the only thing he could do. He closed his eyes, and prayed the end was fast and painless! Had no idea what it was like to die. He wasn't sure if he believed in Heaven or Hell. He said a prayer, regardless, and hoped if there was a God that the Big Man was listening. He knew the only way he'd survive the raptors attack was by a miracle. And everyone knew miracles didn't happen.

CHAPTER 21

Gunfire exploded from all around. Bullets whipped through the air. Powell heard the hiss of them passing close to his face. Rounds of ammo slammed into the velociraptors. Blood and brain matter sprayed from holes in prehistoric skulls. Both raptors crashed forward. Powell threw his hands up, ignoring the pain that radiated through his right arm.

The crushing weight of the raptors on top of him made it impossible to move. He thought ribs might snap under the weight. He strained, wiggling left and right, using the heel of his boots to push in the mud. If the ground had been hard, it might be easier squeezing out from under the beasts. Right now, he thought he might actually be sinking into a suffocating grave.

"Hold on, man. Hang in there. You hurt?" John Marksman stood above him.

Miracles. "I'm okay. I broke my arm. Maybe a rib."

Marksman grunted out a laugh. "You're breathing, brother. That's what counts right now."

"You two gonna kiss, or wanna give me a hand pushing one of these bad boys off of him," Ian Ross said.

# # #

"I hate long hellos more than I hate long goodbyes," Ross said. "We have maybe an hour of daylight left. That's it."

Marksman spoke to Ruh.

Ruh nodded when Marksman finished. He stepped forward and hugged Powell and Claire.

"I told him to go home," Marksman said. "We'll either make it to the river or we won't. No sense endangering the boy. Kid was far braver than I could have imagined. I barely said hello to any of them at the pit. They were just dumb natives to me. I didn't look at them as people. Is that shallow or what?"

Powell used Ian's bandana to create a makeshift sling for his right arm. He gave Claire the rifle. Marksman showed her how to use it. Armed, and ready, they began cutting a way through the forest.

They worked themselves into a pretty good pace. They stayed single file. Marksman on point, Ian in the back of the line. No spot in the order was safer than the other. Marksman made it clear that the gunshots fired would attract more raptors. They had to keep moving, and move fast.

"They're trackers," Marksman had said. "Seems like once they pick up our scent, they can find us anywhere."

Powell had told them about the shaman at the village.

"Mumbo jumbo," was what Ian called the ceremony.

It seemed to work protecting the village. Maybe the dinosaurs didn't like the odor of that particular burning leaf. There was no point arguing, or even discussing any of it at the moment. They had a goal; a target.

Reaching the river *was* obtainable.

Powell breathed in and out, short, shallow breaths. Every time his foot hit the ground, pain radiated inside his chest and sprayed through his arm. Ignoring the pain was not an option, working through it was the only thing he could do.

They ran faster, and faster, as if Marksman could actually see a light at the end of the tunnel.

Powell clung onto hope, again. He hoped he wasn't foolish for doing so. He hoped the four of them would make it alive out of the Congo.

The river must be close.

The river—

The long guttural growling and screeching roar echoed throughout the valley they'd descended into. The ear splitting sounds echoed off of trees and rocks. Like the last few times, he couldn't pinpoint where the velociraptor was, or if there was more than one calling out.

"It's there!" Marksman was shouting. "The river! It's right ahead!"

The backpack felt like bricks in a bag over Powell's back. He pressed a hand against his side. It was a shooting pain. He remembered getting the same thing when he ran distance on the track around the football field at the high school. He was cramping up. Now was not the time.

Powell's hands felt naked without the rifle in his grip. He was defenseless.

He heard gunshots ring out from behind him. Ian must have the raptors in his sight. Powell was almost bent forward running. His side ached. He did not stop, but actually ran a little faster.

Ian was letting out roars of his own as he fired the rifle. He sounded more like a lion, as if he thought *he* was king of the jungle.

He might have been in some jungles. Not in this one.

Powell saw it. The river was brown. It could have been fast flowing mud. It didn't matter. That would still be a better alternative to trudging their way over an unbeaten path in the middle of nowhere.

But where was a boat?

They still had to find a boat.

Marksman stopped on the river bank. He turned and fired his assault rifle. He waved Claire forward, encouraging her not to stop. "Go," he said, "Go, jump!"

Jump?

Claire plunged into the river.

Powell couldn't see her any longer. The current looked powerful. Could she even swim?

"Move it, Powell! Move it!" Marksman was shouting over the din of steady machine gun fire. "Into the river!"

Powell didn't hear shots from behind any longer.

He did hear the unmistakable sound of branches snapping and cracking and splintering.

Was Ian dead? Had the raptors gotten him?

Powell made it just feet from the river bank. Marksman looked like he was shooting to take off Powell's head. Powell even threw up an arm. It was a useless gesture. It just seemed better than having his face blown clean off.

"Into the river!"

Powell didn't need to be told twice.

He heard jaws snap just behind his head as his feet left the ground and he was in the air.

The rushing water was cool. He sank like a rock. He could hear the bubbles racing toward the surface all around him. He swam with them using his arms and kicking his legs.

When his head breached, he looked around for signs of...anything. He was turned around. He didn't know left from right. East from West. He couldn't find Marksman on the bank. He let the current carry him while he scanned the water for Claire.

He ignored the sick feeling in his stomach that anacondas and crocodiles were below and about to eat him feet first. It couldn't be like jumping from the fire into the frying pan, or could it?

He saw a boat. He didn't believe it, but there it was. The small dock it was tied to held one other surprise. Claire was by the pillar in the water. She held onto it with both hands. She had to be exhausted. Fighting the current would spend too much energy. He swam with the current toward Claire.

A smile spread across her face when she saw him.

He reached the dock and grabbed onto the pillar beside her. "Holy shit," was what he said.

"Now what?"

"We borrow this boat," Powell said.

"Where's Ian, and John?"

"Let's get in the boat. Climb up my back onto the dock," Powell said.

She looked like she might resist the command, but wordlessly climbed his back. She stayed on her belly and reached down with her hand. She helped lift him out of the water.

"Get in the boat, I'll untie her," Powell said.

"Louis," she said.

"What?"

The fear lit behind her eyes was a tell. Powell turned around.

A raptor ran at them from across a small clearing. Nothing but open space, and it was headed right for them.

"Get in the boat," Powell said, pulling at the ropes. The knots were fucking tight. He had no idea how they were tied. Were they like Navy knots? In the Congo? Using mostly one hand wasn't helping.

"Hurry, Louis, hurry!"

Powell refused to look back. "Start the engine, Claire," he said and motherfucked the craftsmanship of the knot.

The engine started immediately.

It didn't matter. They were running out of time. The raptor was almost there, and it let out a roar of warning, or as an early victory cry. Either way, it shot shivers throughout Powell's spine.

"Get in the boat, Louis," Claire said.

"I have to untie these," he demanded.

"In the boat. Now!"

Powell didn't look back, but dove into the boat.

He heard a metallic clank, and the boat was free. Claire's machete was buried in the wood on the dock. The current pulled the boat away from the dock, but in what felt like slow motion.

The raptor didn't stop. It ran to the edge of the dock and fell into the river.

Claire screamed.

"I didn't think they could swim!" Powell shouted.

The raptor went under. Its nose rose above water for a moment, and then disappeared.

"Is it under us?" Claire looked over the side of the boat. Her entire body was shivering.

Powell sighed. "There it is," he said, pointing. The velociraptor had made it to the bank and was futilely attempting to scurry out of the water, and then they rounded a bend in the river and it seemed like their nightmare might finally be over.

Something slammed into the side of the boat.

Claire screamed, and Powell jumped back. The boat rocked.

Hands clapped onto the sides.

It took a moment for that to register, that it was hands and not talons. He rushed forward and knelt leaning over the side.

Marksman winked at them. "You gonna stare at me, or help me into the boat? Give me a hand, will ya?"

EPILOGUE

The three of them made it out of the Congo alive.

Powell and Claire resigned from Circuitz. Not a week later, they both died in a tragic car accident. They were in the Pocono region on their way to New York City for a well-deserved vacation.

John Marksman took a sabbatical from mercenary work and wrote a book that topped the New York Times bestseller list. His novel was published as fiction and displayed throughout bookstores across the country.

A handful of people knew the truth.

Some allowed the book to go to print as long as it remained a fictional tale, while the others wanted it removed from shelves, and the author silenced...forever.

Using a phony passport, Marksman disappeared. He left the grid. The only one who knew his whereabouts was his literary agent.

But *they* knew about her, as well.

 SEVERED**PRESS**

CHECK OUT OTHER GREAT DINOSAUR THRILLERS

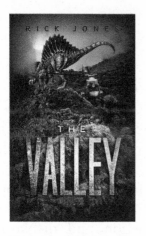

THE VALLEY
by Rick Jones

In a dystopian future, a self-contained valley in Argentina serves as the 'far arena' for those convicted of a crime. Inside the Valley: carnivorous dinosaurs generated from preserved DNA. The goal: cross the Valley to get to the Gates of Freedom. The chance of survival: no one has ever completed the journey. Convicted of crimes with little or no merit, Ben Peyton and others must battle their way across fields filled with the world's deadliest apex predators in order to reach salvation. All the while the journey is caught on cameras and broadcast to the world as a reality show, the deaths and killings real, the macabre appetite of the audience needing to be satiated as Ben Peyton leads his team to escape not only from a legal system that's more interested in entertainment than in justice, but also from the predators of the Valley.

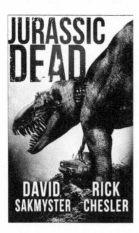

JURASSIC DEAD
by Rick Chesler & David Sakmyster

An Antarctic research team hoping to study microbial organisms in an underground lake discovers something far more amazing: perfectly preserved dinosaur corpses. After one thaws and wakes ravenously hungry, it becomes apparent that death, like life, will find a way.

Environmental activist Alex Ramirez, son of the expedition's paleontologist, came to Antarctica to defend the organisms from extinction, but soon learns that it is the human race that needs protecting.

CHECK OUT OTHER GREAT
DINOSAUR THRILLERS

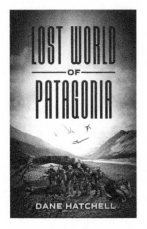

LOST WORLD OF PATAGONIA
by Dane Hatchell

An earthquake opens a path to a land hidden for millions of years. Under the guise of finding cryptid animals, Ace Corporation sends Alex Klasse, a Cryptozoologist and university professor, his associates, and a band of mercenaries to explore the Lost World of Patagonia. The crew boards a nuclear powered All-Terrain Tracked Carrier and takes a harrowing ride into the unknown.

The expedition soon discovers prehistoric creatures still exist. But the dangers won't prevent a sub-team from leaving the group in search of rare jewels. Tensions run high as personalities clash, and man proves to be just as deadly as the dinosaurs that roam the countryside.

Lost World of Patagonia is a prehistoric thriller filled with murder, mayhem, and savage dinosaur action.

SAVAGE ISLAND
by Alan Spencer

Somewhere in the Atlantic Ocean, an uncharted island has been used for the illegal dumping of chemicals and pollutants for years by Globo Corp's. Private investigator Pierce Range will learn plenty about the evil conglomerate when Susan Branch, an environmentalist from The Green Project, hires him to join the expedition to save her kidnapped father from Globo Corp's evil hands.

Things go to hell in a hurry once the team reaches the island. The bloodthirsty dinosaurs and voracious cannibals are only the beginning of the fight for survival. Pierce must unlock the mysteries surrounding the toxic operation and somehow remain in one piece to complete the rescue mission.

Ratchet up the body count, because this mission will leave the killing floor soaked in blood and chewed up corpses. When the insane battle ends, will there by anybody left alive to survive Savage Island?

Made in the USA
Las Vegas, NV
20 December 2022